The limousine and plunged into the trees at the side of the road, tried and failed to climb an old one, caromed off in a backward fling, wedged itself driver's-side-down between two others.

Bolan was already clear of his own vehicle and feeding another round of HE into the '79. He sent it on ahead, this time with maximum effect. The armored hood to the engine compartment had sprung open, also a rear door. The HE impacted directly on target to lay another wreath of fire around the now vulnerable vehicle. It shuddered briefly, then gasoline vapors inside the engine compartment ignited.

Bolan closed immediately, but warily, circling for the best firing line into that blackened doorway.

But the time for caution was past.

He counted four bodies in there, clothing smouldering on two in the rear, broken heads and bloody renderings mutely crying the fate of the two in front.

There should have been six, in there.

He threw a glance along the backtrack, pursed his lips in silent thought, then clipped the '79 to his leg, closed the raincoat on it, and set off, on foot, toward Central Park West.

It was probably going to be a damned long day.

The Executioner Series:

WRITE FOR OUR FREE CATALOG

If there is a Pinnacle Book you want—and you cannot find it locally—it is available from us simply by sending the title and price plus 50¢ per order and 10¢ per copy to cover mailing and handling costs to:

Pinnacle Books, Inc.
Reader Service Dept.
2029 Century Park East
Los Angeles, California 90067

Please allow 4 weeks for delivery. New York State and California residents add applicable sales tax.

_____Check here if you want to receive our catalog regularly.

the EXECUTIONER

#38

SATAN'S SABBATH

by Don Pendleton

PINNACLE BOOKS   LOS ANGELES

This is a work of fiction. All the characters and events portrayed in this book are fictional, and any resemblance to real people or incidents is purely coincidental.

EXECUTIONER #38: SATAN'S SABBATH

Copyright © 1980 by Don Pendleton

All rights reserved, including the right to reproduce this book or portions thereof in any form.

An original Pinnacle Books edition, published for the first time anywhere.

First printing, March 1980

ISBN: 0-523-40338-0

Cover illustration by Gil Cohen

Printed in the United States of America

PINNACLE BOOKS, INC.
2029 Century Park East
Los Angeles, California 90067

My friends, these people whom you see,
are the last obstacle which stops us
from being where we have so long struggled
to be. We ought, if we could, to eat
them up alive.
—Xenophon, *Anabasis*

God himself took a day to rest in, and
a good man's grave is his Sabbath.
—John Donne, *Sermons*

Forget it; this Sabbath has been
claimed by the devil. Let's just go
eat them up alive!
—Mack Bolan, *The Executioner*

This book is dedicated to the
hardcore faithful who have been
in measured step behind the man
since that terrible moment at
Pittsfield when his Awakening
and his War began.
To all of you, to each of you,
our gratitude and respect.

SATAN'S SABBATH

PROLOGUE

The final page from Mack Bolan's war journal:

It is an entropic universe, therefore life itself is a paradox. So I guess it is not so strange that the large events of an individual lifetime are themselves paradoxical. Such as death. This final event should be a dissolution, an entropic spread, a final loss of focus. Yet, poised at this moment upon my final threshold, I am aware that my life is focused as it has never been before. I am now at the pinpoint of all that I have ever been, done, desired, feared. It is a painful focus, yes. But I can bear it. I must bear it. It contains all that I am.

CHAPTER 1

ROLES

It was a misty, blustery morning in midtown Manhattan when the tall man in the hot Ferrari sports car cruised slowly past the UN Plaza and circled via FDR Drive to an apartment complex overlooking the East River. He left the vehicle at the curb in the portico of a luxury highrise, snapped icy eyes at the doorman and handed him a twenty dollar bill, growled, "Watch the car," and went inside to confront his destiny.

The confrontation came in a tenth floor, riverview apartment. Present were Leo Turrin—until recently underboss and de facto head of a western Massachusetts crime family, now a rising power in the administrative arm of *La Commissione*, central governing body of worldwide Mafia operations; one Billy Gino, once Captain of Arms (Head Cock) for the now defunct Marinello Family which, at its height, controlled the city of New York and, by logical extension, all crime territories everywhere; Johnny Grazzi, an up and coming challenger for strutting rights in the Brooklyn territory; plus a nervous retinue of bodycocks and tagmen who had accompanied their respective lords to the secret parley above the East River.

The tall man with the icy eyes had developed a fearsome reputation as "Omega"—one of the nameless, faceless "super enforcers" of the international gestapo who carry playing cards as their only identification—aces all—and Omega was an "Ace of Spades"—the death card—a man who, it was rumored, could hit even a *capo* on his own authority, if such drastic action could be defended before the ruling council of crime kings.

Billy Gino was one of those middle-generation *Mafiosi* who could remember the good old days of fealty and brotherhood within Mafia ranks, a man given to nostalgic wishes and romantic impulses. He virtually worshipped Omega as a symbol of those lost days. On this occasion, he could barely restrain himself from kissing the hand of this awesome Black Ace; in fact, he did, though symbolically—kissing his

2

own as a substitute courtesy, perhaps unconsciously, as he greeted the great man.

Grazzi knew Omega by reputation only, having just recently ascended to the ranks of power within the decimated organization—decimated by the relentless warfare of a one-man army named Mack Bolan. In a sense, then, Grazzi owed his present status in the outfit to Bolan. But it was a debt which could be paid only with Grazzi's own blood . . . and he knew that Bolan would be only too happy to accept the payment. It was this knowledge which had brought Grazzi to the meeting above the East River. Mack Bolan, it was said, was coming back. With blood in his eye. Another Bolan assault against New York would mean one of two things for Johnny Grazzi: either Grazzi would die . . . or he would rise even higher in the new power vacuum produced by Bolan's third sweep of the New York territories.

Johnny Grazzi was not ready to die.

So he was very happy indeed to be invited to this secret meeting with the legendary Ace of Spades, though he probably had as much to fear from Omega as from Mack Bolan.

Leo Turrin was his usual, noncommittal self —a handsome man in his early thirties—apparently relaxed but generating an inner tension which could be felt by a perceptive observer.

The four repaired to a conference table behind locked doors—leaving the assortment of

3

gunbearers to gaze suspiciously at one another in an outer room—and Omega called the meeting to order with a terse announcement: "We're going to keep it simple and to the point."

"Only way to go," replied Turrin, speaking around a fat cigar.

"Just what is the point?" inquired Grazzi, shifting his gaze in an effort to encompass all three of his companions.

"Ask Billy," said Omega.

Billy Gino bit nervously at his lower lip as he locked gazes with Grazzi. "I've had it," he intoned solemnly, "with legless bosses. Present company excepted, there's not a man left in the outfit with real legs to stand on. I don't, uh, include myself in that 'present company' bit, of course. I've never been a boss and I've never wanted to be. But it's guys like me that get chopped up in the service of legless bosses. The thing has been going to hell steadily since Augie Marinello lost his legs in Jersey. And it fell apart completely, far as I'm concerned, when he lost the rest of his body at Pittsfield. Now you all know what I went through with David Eritrea. I'm just here to say that I don't intend to go through something like that again. Especially not if Mack Bolan is looking us over and licking his chops again. That's all I got to say."

"Well said," commented Turrin, nodding his head.

4

Grazzi quietly asked, "Who says Bolan is looking at us again?"

Omega took that one. "We're being told that common sense says it. We're asked to look at the pattern. Today is Saturday—right? The Chicago combine bought it on Monday. Los Angeles fell on Tuesday. Wednesday was the desert fiasco. Thursday, Florida. Baltimore yesterday. What did I say it is here in New York? —Saturday?"

Grazzi shifted uncomfortably on his chair and said, "You can't tie all that to Bolan, can you? I mean—okay, the guy is hell on wheels —but he's still a human being. Right? How could one human being raise all that much hell in just five days? I mean—let's be reasonable. How could he do it?"

"With a little help, maybe," said Omega, quietly.

"From who?"

Omega shrugged his shoulders and lit a cigarette, relaxed into his chair, blew smoke at the ceiling. "I can tell you that *some*one we all know was in the desert on Tuesday. That same someone was in Baltimore yesterday. And I happen to know that this same Mr. Coincidence was tied in on the Colorado thing, way back, and that he had his fingers in the jam at Los Angeles."

Grazzi frowned and said, "Your Mr. Coincidence is also known as Marco Minotti?"

"The same," Omega confirmed, sighing.

"So what are you saying?"

"I'm just wondering, Johnny. As we all should. Things being as they are."

Turrin observed, "Marco came a long way in a short time. We all know that. Not to compare with you, Johnny. You've been solid for a long time—with good legs and feet under you for as long as I've known you. But what was Marco when Augie bought it? Huh? He was peddling numbers in the Bronx for his brother, Frank."

"And Frank," Billy Gino added, with disgust in his voice, "went down in Augie's crash. Nobody yet has been able to sift through all that hanky-pank. We still don't know exactly who did what to who."

"Or why," Turrin said sourly.

Grazzi, with furrowed brow, drummed his fingers on the table and said, "Let me get this straight. You're saying that Marco got his legs from . . . from *Mack Bolan*, f'God's sake?"

No one replied to that, for a moment. Then Omega turned his gaze to the window and said, very quietly, "We haven't said that, yet, Johnny. We are saying that some one should be wondering about it. Especially now, with Marco beating new drums about another Bolan sweep."

"We mean," said Turrin, "like . . . maybe this Bolan has been greatly overrated. Purposely, maybe. Maybe he's been getting a lot of credit that he doesn't really own."

6

"Like, maybe," said Omega, "you're right, Johnny, and the guy could not possibly have hit Indiana on Monday, Los Angeles on Tuesday, White Sands on Wednesday, Florida on Thursday, and Baltimore on Friday. But we all know that all those territories certainly did get hit. And we're wondering—like you, Johnny—we're wondering if one man could have done all that. We're wondering, even, if this Mack Bolan is still alive." Omega sent another blast of smoke toward the ceiling. "Or if he ever was."

Grazzi got to his feet and went to the window, hands jammed into pants pockets, his face darkly troubled.

"Did you ever see the guy, Johnny?" Omega quietly inquired.

"No I never did."

"Do you *know* anybody who ever did?"

"No I guess I don't, at that."

Billy Gino said, "Well, of course, beg your pardon but the guy never left any walking wounded behind. Them that saw him didn't live to tell about it."

"Billy's right," said Turrin. "But not a hundred percent. You're forgetting, Omega, that Bolan started out with me. I'm not that anxious to remind everybody how I got suckered by the guy but I have to say that I knew him like a brother and that he actually exists. Or *did*."

"That was a long time ago," Omega pointed out.

"That's right, it was."

7

"Could the guy have lasted this long? *Any* guy. With a million dollars in bounties on his head and with every cop in the country after his ass? We need to ask ourselves—and right now—"

Turrin interrupted to say, "My uncle Sergio was the first boss to bite Bolan's dust. He used to rage and storm at us, when Bolan was making us all look like a bunch of saps—Sergio used to say to us that one man alone could not be doing all this. He thought the feds were behind it all. He thought they'd invented Mack Bolan just as a cover to hide behind—that he was really many guys, all feds. They couldn't get to us legally so they were doing it with a myth. Of course, he was wrong. Bolan hit the Most Wanted list right away and he's been there ever since. But I have to wonder, too, Omega . . . could the guy be long dead and buried somewhere in a cement coffin. And could someone else now be using his reputation to cover all the shitty things that have been happening to us lately."

"So," said Omega, "we're back to where we started. I said that we should keep it simple and to the point. Johnny wanted to know just what was the point. So this is the point. Marco says that Bolan is going to hit us again. Today, maybe. Soon, for sure. So says Marco. And he says that we should all rally to his banner. The question I'm asking is simple and to the point. Should we do that? Should we all put our guns

8

and our lives into the hands of Marco Minotti? That's about as pointed as I can get. Is Marco the new Boss of Bosses?"

Grazzi returned to the table and took his seat. He placed his right hand on the center of the table, palm down, and very quietly said, "Marco is not *Capo di tutti Capi.*"

Leo Turrin placed his right hand atop Grazzi's. Billy Gino, with only the slightest hesitation, added his own to the stack.

Omega, instead, got to his feet and went to the window. From there, he told them, "You know that I can't add my hand to that pact. I serve the Blessed Thing, not the men who make it. You men make it blessed again. And I will serve it again."

Billy Gino wept openly.

Johnny Grazzi had a faraway look in his eyes, thinking perhaps of glory days ahead.

Leo Turrin just looked solemn. With good reason. Leo was a long-emplaced federal undercover operative as well as close friend and loyal ally to Mack Bolan.

Omega looked solemn, also, with even better reason. Omega was Mack Bolan.

CHAPTER 2

IDENTIFICATION

Mack Bolan was a human being, yes—not a killer robot nor a perpetual-motion military machine. Even in the real war zones—those hellgrounds called Southeast Asia—Sergeant Bolan, for all his splendid military achievements, had been regarded as nothing more than a dedicated warrior and superb militarist. Though he earned there his nickname, The Executioner, not once during two full combat tours behind enemy lines was there an accusation or even a hint that the death specialist was "out of control" or tainted in any way by military excess.

Indeed, Sergeant Bolan earned another nickname among the villagers of those wartorn lands who called him, in their own tongue, the equivalent of "Sergeant Mercy"—a name which became legend among forward medics and Special Forces teams who were the first to move into "pacified" areas where Bolan had been operating.

He had initially entered the combat theatre as an armor specialist and volunteer advisor in the effort to equip and train the fierce Montagnard tribesmen. Eventually he found himself with a small team of American specialists who worked with the Montagnards in an operation called "Project Backburn," designed to counter VC hit and run terrorism in the no-man's-land regions of Vietnam. Later, due to his experience with Backburn, Bolan was selected as the first experimental "death specialist," provided with a five-man support team, and charged with missions to pursue enemy terrorists into sanctuary areas (though these assignment rarely found their way into the official record). This group, officially but loosely attached to the Ninth Infantry as "Penetration Team Able," became the prototype for other operational groups which, it is said, later evolved into (or became synonymous with) the "Black Berets" or LRRP's (Long Range Reconnaissance Patrols). Whatever the official organizational line, PenTeam Able survived as a separate entity, for all operational purposes, and Sergeant Mack Bolan became a quiet legend among military and civilian communities alike. It is said that there is more to the Mack Bolan story in secret CIA files than in any military record—and it seems likely that Sergeant Bolan would have died a quiet hero's death somewhere in the steamy interiors of Vietnam or Cambodia (considering the nature of his work) except for the intervention of tragedy at home.

Bolan was sent home on compassionate leave to bury his mother, his father, and a 17-year-old sister—and to arrange for the care of an orphaned 14-year-old brother.

He never returned to Southeast Asia.

Sergeant Bolan had found a larger war, much closer to home, and a far more menacing enemy than anything encountered in the savage jungles of Vietnam. Sergeant Bolan found the Mafia. And he declared war everlasting upon them.

The details of this new war are not buried in secret CIA files. They are a matter of public record, because Mack Bolan quickly became a public figure. His own unique brand of blazing and unrelenting warfare was not to be contained by governmental policies, not for this war, nor was it to be confused by conventional morals or politics. Bolan had found, also, a "higher morality" and "political sanity." Stripped to its essentials, this new understanding simply stated that savages shall not be allowed to dominate civilized peoples and that no "cure" is too harsh to insure a solution to the problem.

Mack Bolan had a "cure" for the Mafia problem.

It would be impossible to say, with any certainty, just how much of this philosophy was bred in the hellgrounds of Vietnam or how much was inspired by Bolan's personal confrontation with the savage reality of Mafia power. It should be noted, however, that Sergeant Mercy prowled the same hellgrounds as The Executioner, at one and the same time, in the same mind and body—and it is a matter of public record that no innocent victims fell to The Executioner's guns in this new War Against the Mafia.

He was not, as some charged, a deranged or embittered casualty of the Vietnam experience, too restless at home and too insensitive to humanitarian ideals to allow the American justice system to run its natural course.

There was, he knew, no way to handle the Mafia problem under the American system of justice.

The savages were winning . . . until Mack Bolan came along.

But he was a human being, yes. He bled like other men, wearied like other men, wept like other men—and he killed, as other men have done down through the ages when they became convinced that the cause was right and desperate.

Mack Bolan was a human being.

He was one hell of a human being.

CHAPTER 3

THE DEADLY GAME

It had been a gross exaggeration, of course. Marco Minotti was not now and had never been a legless wonder but was a vicious shark in Mafia waters from his earliest beginnings as a gunbearer for his brother, Frank, a lieutenant in the old Marinello outfit. Nor had he merely "peddled numbers" in the Bronx but had taken that territory for himself in a bloodless coup which sent two older mafiosi into premature retirement in Florida.

True, Marco had used his brother's name as a lever for many of his early successes with the family business—but by the time of Augie Marinello's death, it had already become quiet speculation, among those in the know, as to just how much longer it might be before Frank, himself, was packed off to a retirement condominium in Miami. Bolan's execution of the elder brother had merely advanced the inevitable to an earlier date—and Marco had lost no time consolidating the remnants of Frank's little empire into a conglomerate pirated from the surviving bits and pieces of the Marinello consortium.

In effect, Marco had succeeded Marinello. Augie had been the boss of bosses. Ergo, Marco should now wear that crown. He had, in fact, been acting as though he did.

Which accounted for Billy Gino's unhappiness with the guy.

As for Johnny Grazzi, certainly he did not share Billy's assessment of the new boss of Manhattan. It was common knowledge, moreover, that Grazzi despised and feared Minotti with passions that spanned the years. So although he did not buy the favorable comparison between himself and a feared enemy, it must have felt nice to get his fur stroked in such strong company. Evidently the stroking had proven sufficient to provoke a commitment of sorts. That was all Bolan had been going for—a state of mind which would be conducive to later manipulation.

It was, after all, a damned game.

A deadly serious one, to be sure—and a terribly important one—but a game, nevertheless.

The conversation in that riverview apartment had been numbingly accurate, in at least one detail. No one man could have ever hoped for such extravagant successes against a worldwide organization of savages such as this one. Unless that one man happened to be a damned good gamesman—and unless he could pick up a few strong friends along the way.

Bolan had been fortunate in both departments. He'd been *trained* as a gamesman, by experts in the biggest game of all, and he had indeed been joined in the game by some of the largest friends a man could have.

"With a little help, maybe," he'd suggested to Grazzi.

Mack Bolan had received a damn lot of help, and he knew it, and it was an item of pride with him.

Not every "human being" in Mack Bolan's world had elected to roll over and play dead for the bully boys. That was, yes, an item of considerable pride.

But it was time, now, to get on with the game. The first move was Bolan's. And he knew exactly where to begin.

Bolan touched a small selenium dot embedded in his left lapel and said to it, "Are you on me?"

April Rose's voice murmured back via a small, thickened area in the frame of his sunglasses. "Loud and clear, Striker. Your wires are firm."

17

Which meant that every word spoken in that apartment had been preserved on tape in the Warwagon's intelligence console.

He told his helpmate: "Track loose. I'll be taking a bath on Central Park West."

She would understand that. And the big GMC motorhome would orbit that next checkpoint, listening to transpiring events and maintaining a support posture in this deadliest of all deadly games.

He smiled grimly to himself and put the Ferrari into the traffic flow.

The last day of the last mile was underway.

The Roman Nights "bathhouse and spa" took pride in the fact that it was open 24 hours a day and that it employed "New York's most beautiful attendants." It was a "private club" which sold memberships in the lobby to anyone with the price—and, of course, all major credit cards were gladly accepted.

The guy at the counter was not particularly beautiful, nor even attractive. He showed Bolan a hideous smile and told him, in a gutteral monotone, "You came at a good time, sport. Day shift just came on, fresh and ready, so you get the choice of the house. You a member?"

Bolan flashed the death card at the guy and said, "Better than that, sport. Is he here?"

The phony smile stayed but the gravelly voice undertook a new strain as the guy replied, "He's never here this early."

"That's the problem," Bolan said, his gaze roaming the empty lobby. He wore a black raincoat over a $500 sharkskin suit, a snapbrim black hat, yellow-tinted lenses in white bone frames, and a face to chill Antarctica. "What's your name?"

"I'm Lou Nola," said the growler, nervously. "I manage the day shift. What's wrong?"

"Who's here?"

"Just me'n the girls, Tony and Jake."

"Who are Tony and Jake?"

"You know, the muscle. What's wrong?"

"No customers?"

"Oh sure, it's early but we got a few. What's wrong?"

Bolan grabbed the guy by an arm and pulled him from behind the counter. "Let's go."

"Where we going?"

"Inside. Quickly. Move it."

The guy moved it, leading Bolan up a curving staircase to where the action was while growling over his shoulder, "What the hell is going on?"

Bolan showed him a solemn smile as he replied, "Right now, Lou, I want a look at your customers."

Nola was beginning to enter the spirit of the thing, whatever it was. His eyes were dancing with excitement as he led Bolan into the second floor lounge. "You never been here before, sir?"

Bolan assured him that he had not.

"Well this's the hots room. The customers can meet the girls here and look 'em over if they don't already have one in mind. We get a lot of repeat business, of course. Class joint. Best girls in town. And we get a classy trade. No ten dollar hand jobs in this place, bet your ass."

The "hots room" had a stale atmosphere, poor lighting, a small self-serve bar in one corner, several large couches, soiled harem pillows strewn about, and a large-screen projection TV being fed nonstop porno from a video tape player.

But the girls were not so bad. Two of them, rather loosely draped in thigh-length garments which probably were supposed to be togas, were at the bar with an arrogant looking muscleman who had to be either Tony or Jake. He wore pants too tight to sit and a red T-shirt with "Get Screwed" emblazoned across the chest.

Nola called the bouncer over and told him, "We're checking the johns. Where are they?"

Tony or Jake, whichever, replied, "Two in the whirlpool with Janie and Paula." He curiously eyed Bolan as he added, "Wilma's balling one upstairs. What's the problem?"

Bolan asked, "How many girls on duty right now?"

"They're all here," the muscleman said coldly.

"Twelve," Nola hastily added, with a rebuking frown at the other.

Bolan commanded that other, "Round up all

the unattached girls and take them out of here. I mean all the way out, across the street, to the park. On the double quick and just as they are."

"I can't take them out there like that, with their asses hanging out! What the hell is—?"

"Just do it!" Bolan snarled, giving the guy a hard shove for emphasis.

Nola cried, "Well wait, I—"

Bolan halted that nervous protest with a throaty growl and a hard look. But the voice was coldly controlled as he told that guy, "This joint is wired to go up in flames. I don't know when. It could be any minute. Show me the baths, then you scout around and make sure everybody gets out of the building."

"A bomb?" Nola gasped.

"Don't waste time with dumb questions. Do like I said!"

"Hey, if the joint's gonna go . . !"

The guy wanted to just run away, and to hell with everyone else. Bolan grabbed two fistfuls of shirtfront and slammed the reluctant manager against the wall beside swinging double doors. "You do exactly like I said!" he commanded. "Make sure everyone gets out!" He jerked his head toward the doors. "Are the baths in there?"

"On through the locker room!" Nola replied, choked with fear and with Bolan's big fists buried, as it were, in his throat.

Bolan flung the guy away with a disgusted

21

growl and went through the swinging doors.

The locker room was clean and antiseptic smelling. Varnished wooden benches lined a double row of lockers. A stack of towels and a large carton containing disposable footwear stood on a table beside a door labelled "Private." At the other side, a single swinging door led to the baths.

In there, three large sunken tubs provided the focus for relaxed frolic, around which were scattered massage tables and miscellaneous toys of the erotic variety. A small room beyond contained a wall-to-wall water bed, at floor level.

On almost any night of the week, these "baths" would undoubtedly be wall-to-wall living flesh, a "spa" in every sense of the word for those who enjoy communal sex and are willing to rent partners. Bolan had no particular grudge against the concept nor took any particular pleasure in disrupting the fun of the two "johns" who were presently cavorting rather self-consciously with the busty young ladies in the center tub.

But it was Saturday and this was New York —and the larger game had already begun.

He threw a stack of towels at the foursome and gave them the message. They departed with proper dispatch, fleeing soundlessly on naked feet and clutching their towels about them. Bolan followed them to the locker room door, then gave it a five count and opened his raincoat.

Affixed by a spring-clip gadget strapped to

the outer right leg just above the knee was a specially modified M-79, a 40mm grenade launcher. In its normal configuration, the '79 looked like a short, fat shotgun, the 14-inch barrel accounting for only half the overall length of the weapon. This one, with a cutdown stock, measured only 20 inches overall. The rear leaf sight had been removed. Now it looked like a long, fat pistol.

The M-79 does not hurl a "hand grenade" but fires a 40 millimeter exploding round which may contain buckshot, flare, gas, smoke or high explosive. The high explosive or "HE" round can be quite devastating, especially in contained areas. In a readybelt at his waist, Bolan carried six HE and several smoke rounds. He backed into the locker room and held the swinging door with his hip as he thumbed in a round of HE and let-it fly toward the tubs, releasing the door in the same moment and dancing back to avoid the shock wave.

The floor moved, in there, and windows exploded. He kicked the door open once again and sent a smoke round to the wall beneath the shattered windows, then moved swiftly through the locker room and into the central lounge.

Lou Nola was disappearing down the stairway to the ground floor. A guy dressed identically to the other bouncer was frantically urging a dishevelled, near-nude couple across the room and toward that stairway.

Bolan concealed the '79 beneath his raincoat

as he yelled at that guy. "Is that everybody?"

"That's it!" the bouncer yelled back.

Bolan watched them to the safety of the ground floor, then he crossed to the ascending stairs and was about to send a firestorm to the third floor landing when some quiver of the psyche stayed the trigger finger and sent the feet, instead, up those stairs.

It had been a damned fortunate quiver, indeed.

A pretty kid who looked far too young to be working in a joint like this was in a small room at the end of the hall. She lay nude and unconscious upon a soiled mattress on the floor and she was in a hell of a mess. The room smelled of vomit and so did the girl, some of it encrusted in her tangled hair.

Bolan draped her across his shoulder and carried her to the second floor lounge. Smoke was puffing into the room from beneath the double doors to the baths. He lay the girl on a couch, stripped off his raincoat and wrapped her in it, then hoisted her again to his shoulder and went down the stairs.

Water was pouring through the ceiling and was already ankle deep in the lobby. The blast in the bathhouse had evidently ruptured a water line. The front door stood open and water was flowing outside.

Bolan had planned to level the joint. Maybe it would level itself, with the small help that he had given it.

A curious crowd was gathering at the edge of the park, across the street, as Bolan exited with his burden, much of the attention seeming to center on the scantily clad young women who stood in mute but agitated contemplation of the flames erupting through the second floor windows.

A nervously indignant Lou Nola scampered to Bolan's side as he crossed the street, eyes shifting rapidly from the weapon in Bolan's hand to the raincoat-draped burden draped across his shoulder.

"You should have left the kid," Nola growled. "What the hell am I supposed to do with her, now?"

"I'll take care of it," Bolan growled back. "Call Marco. Tell him what happened."

"He sure ain't gonna like it," Nola said quietly. "Roman Nights was his favorite toy. He ain't gonna like it a bit."

"That," said Bolan, coldly, "is the whole idea, sport." He pushed the guy aside and went on to his car, carefully placed the unconscious girl inside, and went away from there.

April Rose whispered in his ear: "Are you clear? Police and firemen are responding."

"I'm clear," Bolan assured her. "Let's rendezvous. I have a casualty aboard."

"Somebody we know?"

"Nobody we know," he replied.

But it could have been. He glanced at the pathetic mess curled into the seat beside him

25

and shuddered. Yeah. That was the hell of it, the tragic commonality of it; she could have been anyone's kid sister.

As it turned out, the girl was the daughter of someone very special—very special, indeed. But Bolan would not learn of that until the morning flames of Saturday had run their course. For now, it was enough to know that the game had begun . . . and that someone else knew it, now, as well.

CHAPTER 4

VECTORS

The fire was out. Only one fire truck remained, also a special unit from the arson squad. Traffic flow along Central Park West had returned to near normal, with the assistance of a traffic detail of cops. Earlier, a SWAT team had cruised through but did not stop. Most of the onlookers had drifted away and the people from Roman Nights had departed in taxicabs, except for Lou Nola, the day manager. Lou had remained behind to try to explain the happening to his boss, Marco Minotti.

It was not a pleasant task. Minotti was an explosive individual, quick tempered and unpredictable. He listened quietly to what Nola had to say but the storm signals were blazing from his eyes throughout that discourse.

When Nola had run out of words, Minotti stomped over to a park bench and kicked it, then again, as edgy bodyguards smiled nervously at one another. But the anger was under control when the boss turned back to Nola. "I didn't send a guy, Lou," he declared coldly. "Especially I did not send an Ace. Those guys don't cut no ice around here any more."

Nola replied, "No sir, I didn't mean to say that you sent him. In fact, he asked for you. I figure he was acting on a tip from somewhere, not sent by you."

Minotti's voice was dangerously calm as he said, "And he took the kid away with 'im, eh?"

"Yes, sir. Said he'd take care of it. Put her in this fire red Ferrari. I figure—"

"Exactly what did this guy look like?"

Nola cracked his knuckles and set his gaze about two inches to the left of the boss's as he replied. "Tall guy, Mr. Minotti. More'n six feet easy—maybe six-two or three. Shoulders enough to fill a doorway. I wisht I could afford his clothes. And he had a . . . he was . . . when he talked, you felt like jumping. You know? Authority, real authority. But very cool. I know he was the genuine article. Showed me his card."

"You ever see one of those cards before?" Minotti growled.

"No, sir. But I knew what it was when I saw it."

"Did you get the number? Did you even think to check it out before you let him waltz in there and take the joint over?"

Nola was developing a cold sweat. He said, "There was no time for—he said a bomb, it could go off any minute. That's all I could think of. It didn't seem no time to be—"

"What'd he look like?"

"I told you, he—you mean his face. Uh, well, cold . . . cold is what I think of. Uh, square— I would say square jaw. Strong chin. Good teeth. Sort of a good looking guy, I guess. I mean, women would think so. He wore sunshades so I couldn't see his eyes but you got the feeling all the time he was staring holes through you. Oh—he has this smile but it's not a smile, if you know what I mean. Christ, sir, he's a Black Ace. What else can I say?"

Minotti's gaze had gone somewhat glassy about midway through that description. It wavered and fell to the ground then he turned about for further contemplation of the park bench. "Did this so-called Ace wear a hat?" he mumbled at the bench.

"Sir?"

Minotti turned his head only and angrily bit the words. "Did he wear a hat?"

"I think so, yessir. Yes he did. Wore it sort of square."

"Sort of military?"

"Military? I guess—well, yeah, all over. I guess that's what I been going for. Now that you mention it, he looked kind of like a soldier in civvies. But damn nice civvies."

Minotti sighed and turned his whole body around, dropped onto the bench, raised both arms to the backrest, crossed his legs. He sat like that for a long moment, staring at the ground.

The bodyguards walked softly about, as though awaiting an explosion.

Nola lit a cigarette and sucked at it hungrily, stealing glances toward the continuing commotion across the street.

Then a torpedo approached with a report on the disaster. Minotti saw him coming and raised expectant eyes. "So?" he asked quietly.

"It wasn't a bomb, Marco."

"What was it, then?"

"They don't know, yet, for sure. But definitely not a bomb. They're digging shrapnel out of the walls, up there. And something is very funny."

"What, funny?"

"They found something that—well it looks like a smoke shell."

"A what?"

"For setting off a smoke screen."

"Son of a bitch!" Minotti exclaimed disgustedly. "A *smoke* screen!"

"There's not really that much damage, either.

Mostly water and smoke. The fire was contained inside the baths."

Minotti rose slowly to his feet, sent a withering look at Lou Nola, and said, "A bomb, huh?"

Nola shrugged his shoulders and spread his hands. "How could anyone know? When a guy yells bomb, you gotta believe it. They evacuated a big office building just up the street two weeks ago, same thing. But no bomb. What can you do?"

Minotti squared off, flexing his shoulders at Nola as he growled, "You don't just run away and leave something I told you to watch. That's what you *don't* do."

"God, she looked terrible. I couldn't drag her out here and lay her on the grass. They would have had her inside an ambulance in nothing flat. I figured you wouldn't want that." Nola saw the storm coming. He shuffled his feet in a nervous little dance on the grass and added, "He's an *Ace*, Mr. Minotti. Said he would take care of her. Hell I'm sure—"

"Bullshit the Ace!" Minotti raged. He reached out with both hands and shook the little man like a rag doll, then threw him to the ground. "Bullshit the bomb, too, you fucking dummy! He suckered you, dammit! He came to snatch the kid! All the rest of it was just for cover! So don't try to tell me . . !" He kicked at Nola and missed, and that served only to increase his rage.

Nola rolled away and scampered to his feet,

trying to find solace behind a bodyguard. The bodyguard slapped him and threw him back into the arena.

Minotti took a step forward, hand raised to smite the cringing Nola, then he checked the swing and swerved about to stalk off toward his limousine.

The retinue took station around him, one of them jogging ahead to slide into the driver's seat and start the engine.

Nola sagged onto a bench, arms folded across his chest, breathing raggedly and watching the departure with wild eyes.

A police car pulled alongside just as the limousine was about to get underway. A big cop in street clothes stepped out from the passenger side and went around to a rear window of the limousine for a word with Minotti. A bodyguard lowered the window and the cop leaned in for the eyeball parley.

"That you, Marco?"

"Hi, Captain. Things must be getting pretty tough to bring you out on a call like this."

"I was in the neighborhood. This one of your joints?"

"I own the building."

"Uh huh. Who you got mad at you, now?"

"You know how it goes, Cap'n. A nut in every woodpile."

"Maybe. But, then, there's this awful rumor. I guess you've heard it."

"What rumor is that?"

"Grapevine has it that Mack Bolan is back in town."

Minotti smiled and said, "Who is Mack Bolan?"

The cop did not give that response the dignity of any reaction whatever. He smiled back and said, "I wasn't really in the neighborhood. Actually, I've been holed up over at SWAT headquarters since midnight. Just waiting."

"Sounds very boring," Minotti replied quietly. "Waiting for what?"

"First blast, let's call it."

"But you're not there, now."

"That's right. Looks like the wait is over, Marco."

Minotti snickered and said, "I don't know what the hell you're talking about."

"Sure you do."

The cop swept his gaze to encompass all the strained faces in that vehicle, then he stepped back, touched two fingers to his forehead in a relaxed salute, and watched the car lurch away.

"Smart bastard!" Minotti fumed.

"Maybe good news, though," observed the head bodycock, from the front seat. "Sounds like they're going to be all over the guy's ass, this time."

"Don't bet on it," the boss growled. "I'm starting to wonder if maybe those guys have started sleeping with the bastard." He took time to light a cigar, then told the bodycock, "Stop at the first phone. Get ahold of Matty. Tell 'im about the red Ferrari. That thing should stick out in any crowd. What a goddamned . . . who would've thought?— we got every damned spot in town covered like molasses, just waiting for the bastard to show his face. So he shows up at Roman Nights, of all places. And what I want to know is, how'd he know about the kid? Huh? How'd he know?"

"You think it's Bolan for sure, then."

"I think we better *think* that way, at least 'til we know for sure."

The wheelman interrupted that conversation with a tense interjection, his eyes glued to the rearview mirror. "Isn't that a red Ferrari back there? 'Bout a block back?"

All heads swivelled to the rear.

"It's a red something," said the bodycock.

"The nervy bastard!" Minotti said quietly, the voice a bare whisper.

"Forget that phone stop!" the bodycock commanded the wheelman. "Take the next turn into the park! All you boys get ready!"

"The nervy bastard," Minotti repeated. "He brought *us* to *him*."

But it was a prayer, not a complaint.

Marco Minotti, the hopeful Boss of all the Bosses, could not have asked for anything sweeter. Mack Bolan's head would serve as the new banner under which all the boys everywhere would joyously gather. And that head was about to fall into Marco's sack.

CHAPTER 5

THE STRETCH

Some minutes earlier, Bolan had transferred the still unconscious girl to a bunk in the Warwagon and instructed April Rose: "Contact Hal and get some quiet medical attention for this kid. If hospitalization is considered necessary then let's do that quietly, too, and with maximum security. If not, I want her kept in some sort of protective custody."

"Who is she?" April wondered.

"I have no idea," Bolan told her. "And I don't know what her situation is. Maybe just a runaway. And maybe not. I have a gut feeling about this kid and I want her handled with all delicacy. Be sure Hal understands that."

"Hal," of course, was Harold Brognola, No. 1 man in the federal war against organized crime. He was also Bolan's staunchest supporter within the establishment. He was in town, also, with a large force of federal marshals, standing-by to lend whatever covert assistance possible in Bolan's final campaign against the Mafia. Tomorrow, hopefully, Bolan would be in Washington to receive an official, if quiet, remission of sins and to launch a new "quick reaction" capability for the U.S. against outside threats to the national security.

Bolan knew fully that, at this moment, Hal Brognola could not care less about the underworld threat in New York. His overriding concern was to keep Mack Bolan alive and healthy until official government sponsorship began. The chief fed had been very much opposed to the six-day finale to Bolan's domestic campaign, had gone along with it most grudgingly, but had committed himself and the full resources of his office to a successful conclusion.

And not just because they were friends but also because the man in the White House had so ordained it. Too damned many ragtag radicals in far too many third and fourth rate nations had joined the sport of pulling Uncle Sam's whiskers, secure in the belief that the mightiest nation on earth would not risk powderkeg confrontations which could engulf the entire world in cataclysmic warfare. Bolan had been perceived, in Washington, as the perfect solution to that sort of problem. But the proposal had presented a moral dilemma for Bolan himself. He had sworn upon his dead parents' graves to eradicate the Mafia from the face of the land— not as an act of vengeance but as recognition of the greatest evil in American life—and, though he had never expected to actually succeed in that promise, he had pledged his very life toward the attainment. So it was with some surprise that he had to agree with Washington's secret assessment of his cumulative effect upon the organized crime problem: the families were crumbling everywhere, suffering from a staggering attrition at the top, their influence waning in the political and business communities, financial fortunes disappearing in huge chunks under Bolan's relentless determination to hit them everywhere it hurt.

Brognola had carried a personal message from the White House to the blitzing, blacksuited warrior. "The President is a very moral man, Striker, so he naturally abhors the need for violent reaction. But he is also a realist. And he understands your kind of war, that type and level of commitment. Right now he is facing a frightening dilemma, very much like your own, on the international scene. The problem there is almost identical to the crime problem here. These terrorist organizations operate in direct contravention to every precept of international law and morals. They are, in every sense of the word, criminals. And they use our

37

own moral sense against us, the same way the mob has always done. The mob hides behind constitutional guarantees. Terrorists hide behind international law, secure in the belief that the U.S. is chained by moral restraint and worldwide public opinion. They've even begun taunting us about our impotency and flaunting their hatred and disrespect before television cameras and in Third World forums. The implications of all this are really frightening, because it's the sort of thing that feeds on itself and builds its own momentum. Next thing you know, there won't be an American consulate anywhere outside the western world. The ultimate consequence will be a total alienation between west and east, racial hatreds unsurpassed in written history, maybe even a holy war to make all the present World War Three scenarios look like war games. Right now Pakistan is building nuclear weapons. India already has them. Nonproliferation treaties to hell, the nuclear club is no longer an exclusive one. If these tensions keep building then sooner or later—probably sooner—some minor power is going to start trying nuclear blackmail. That's as certain as death. So you can see the dilemma. What the hell can we do to reassert American prestige? How do we prevent the half-civilized world from dominating the responsible powers? The answer, the only answer within reach, is that we have got to stop the terrorism before it reaches epidemic proportions. It may already be too late. We cannot invade those countries which shelter the terrorists, even though we know that in many cases the terrorists are carrying out the will of hostile governments. So—and this is the President's own thinking—we need your brand of solution, Striker. Direct action, forceful and effective, dramatically focused directly onto the perpetrators of crimes against the United States. We cannot bomb a city of a million innocent souls to get at a hundred or so international criminals. But we could do it your way. The President wants you. He wants you immediately."

That was the message.

But the President had found it necessary to accept a compromise, in recognition of Bolan's own moral imperatives. Brognola had carried back the response: "Striker respectfully accepts the commission, sir. But he has a dilemma of his own. He is not fully convinced that the mob is down for the full count. He wants a six-day delay in reporting. He feels an obligation to go the second mile."

"The second what?" inquired the President.

"Like in the Bible, Mr. President. If a man asks you to walk a mile with him—"

"Go with him twain," quoted the President, sighing.

"Yes, sir. You see, back in the beginning, when he first declared this personal war of his, he thought of it as the last mile of a condemned man. Never really thought it would go so well.

39

But, as we all know, that 'last mile' has encompassed the globe. He still can't believe that his war is won, though. And he wants an official commitment by the government. He wants our solemn pledge that we will never again allow the Mafia problem to get out of hand. I gave him that, in your name."

"But he still," said the man behind the oval desk, "insists upon this second-mile effort."

"Yes, sir. His plan is to hit the remaining power centers, six territories in six days. It sounds like a hell of a bite, I know, but I think he just might manage it. I will give him all possible covert support. And, uh, of course we will have to bend the law a bit, here and there, to do so. But I regard it as a justifiable trade-off. On that, I would be willing to take my chances before a responsible jury of American citizens."

"So would I," the chief declared, smiling solemnly.

"Does that mean I have a go, sir?"

"It means," said the President, "that you are to deliver the man to this office one week from today, alive and well. Use your own discretion as how best to accomplish that. We, uh, cannot give him a public pardon, of course. We cannot even publicly acknowledge his official presence in government service. But we can re-create him. And I fully intend to do so. Give him my personal assurances, in that regard."

Brognola had given Bolan just that, along

40

with a full account of the official conversation.

And, yes, Bolan knew that the staggering families of the New York crime council were very low on Brognola's list of priorities. But he also respected Brognola's professional ethics and felt confidence in the calibre of support which could be expected. So he'd left the ailing waif on Brognola's official doorstep with no misgivings whatever. Then he'd returned directly to the firing line, hoping that Minotti the Wolfman would venture there, also.

And, of course, he had.

Bolan paced the Ferrari into a calculated track, inviting attention, and he knew immediately when it came. The big limousine swerved ever so slightly, drifting briefly across the centerline then leaping back to the proper position. A good wheelman would never drive so carelessly with the boss aboard, not unless severely distracted by something larger than the usual driving responsibilities.

So, yes, Bolan knew that he had been spotted, even before that other vehicle lunged east on 96th and into Central Park. He pressed ahead, then, hoping to reach that intersection before the other car could lose itself in the winding park roads. But they were not running away, that much quickly became obvious. They did not wish to lose that red Ferrari, it seemed. When Bolan rounded the turn into Central Park, the limousine was idling near the first intersection inside. As soon as he appeared, they accelerated and turned back south on the park roadway.

Bolan stomped the accelerator and pressed on, smiling grimly and threading a silencer onto the Beretta. This was not really his style, going for hot contact in an uncontrolled environment, but it was an extraordinary time and he felt that the opportunity for a quick score was too important to dismiss out of hand. If he could find some combat stretch—meaning, a clear zone free of innocent bystanders—then certainly he had to press the attack. If not . . . then he would dog their trail and play the ear. But the chances for combat stretch seemed excellent. It was not that great a day to encourage idling in the park. Sporadic rain, mists, and blustery winds were all working in Bolan's favor. A few joggers were out; here and there a cyclist—but no throngs or even clusters.

He found the stretch near the western extremity of Central Park Lake, where wind-driven mists would discourage the most persistent parkers, and leapt forward quickly to within fifty feet of the cruising limousine, then extended the Beretta from the open window and sighted through the windshield to send a silent round into the left rear tire.

It scored, he knew, because he could see the pop of moisture leap from the rubber, but there was no effect.

Bullet-proof tires, uh huh. Which probably

meant that the entire vehicle embodied one of those new, lightweight protective systems which had recently become so popular in this age of terrorist activity.

Unlike the armor-clad behemoths of yesterday, so weighted down with heavy steel panels, these new armored cars were much more secure and not at all obvious. Bolan had some of the stuff incorporated into his own battle cruiser, and he knew its strengths as well as its weaknesses.

The Ferrari, of course, was nothing but weaknesses all the way, in a contest such as this.

But now was the time, and perhaps the only place of this day.

He had to go for it.

And so he went.

CHAPTER 6

TO KILL A TANK

As they made the turn at 96th, head bodycock Joe Salerno was making all the decisions and setting the strategy. At such times, this was not only his right but his charged responsibility. No matter how streetwise a boss may be, it simply made better sense to have a specialist see to such things. A boss could, of course, override the bodycock and take charge for himself—but such bosses were not known for longevity. So Marco's protest was feeble and perfunctory when Salerno ordered the vehicle halted and Minotti out.

"Cut back through the park to the avenue, Marco," he advised. "Jimmy will go with you.

Get a cab and go to the quiet spot. We'll contact you there."

The maneuver was accomplished smoothly and well before the red Ferrari showed up again in the rearview. Minotti and his personal bodyguard disappeared into the shrubbery, the limousine idled along to the next intersection, and then the payday action began.

Counting his own, Salerno had four hot guns inside that car. It was a veritable tank of the boulevards. Tires, gas tank, and all the glass could handle a sustained assault by a dozen machine guns. The body was virtually impregnable, even the underside. There were protected gunports in the rear seat area and in the passenger side up front as well as special defensive and evasive systems to neutralize pursuit—though, of course, there was now no desire to discourage pursuit.

The wheelman growled, "Here he comes."

The Ferrari was starting to crowd the rear.

Salerno winked solemnly at the left rear gunner. The guy opened his gunport and slipped the muzzle of an Uzi submachine gun through the portal.

"He's got a bean shooter," said the other gunner, noting a pistol that had appeared outside the Ferrari.

Salerno snickered as a pencilflame appeared back there and a barely noticeable pop came from a rear tire. "Silencer, yet," he observed. "Come on, guy, you can do better than that."

The wheelman tensely inquired, "Should I hit the oil slick?"

"Hell no!" Salerno quickly replied. "Make him come around!"

"He's coming!" reported the left gunner, like an echo. A second later: "Well shit! What's that?"

The window on the passenger side of the Ferrari was down. A strange looking weapon with a barrel wide enough to shoot golfballs was resting in the open window.

"That's a grenade launcher!" the wheelman cried.

"Easy, easy," Salerno growled.

These boys did not really know how secure this car was. For that matter, neither did Salerno. He'd read all the engineering reports, of course, and knew what it was *designed* to withstand but there had never been an acid test with Joe Salerno inside.

Salerno himself would have greatly desired a proof run with someone, anyone, other than Mack Bolan doing the proving. But here they were. And there was the guy the whole mob had been itching for since forever. Joe could see him as clear as looking into his own mirror. And he'd seen that face before, sure, somewhere. An involuntary tremor traveled his spine and tickled both ears. The red Ferrari was coming around, the guy driving with one hand while the other extended that impressive weapon through the window opening.

"He's headed for the grass!" the wheelman warned.

Salerno flung his hand at the rear gunner and yelled, "Open fire!"

It was the last thing any of them heard, for a while. The chatter of the Uzi was magnified tenfold within the tightly enclosed environment of that armored vehicle, battering the ears and assaulting all the senses with the near-unbearable racket.

But Salerno could see all right. He could see the line of holes sprouting in that hot little car alongside, could see window-glass shattering, could see the flash of red arcing away as the Ferrari plunged into the park and ran ahead, then came back around broadside, passenger side to.

For an instant, then—for one terrible, heart-stopping instant, all Joe Salerno could see was the golfball-size barrel blowing flame from that window, a flame which magnified instantly to engulf his own windshield in a fiery mushroom.

And that, probably, was the last thing Joe Salerno saw.

It was a long shot, he knew—certainly not an odds play with which any thinking man would be comfortable. But he also knew that winning plays, in this kind of game, were not necessarily the cautious ones.

He saw the snout of the Uzi projecting from the gunport and knew that he would have to run a gauntlet of murderous fire, at almost point-blank range. That was not comforting. He knew, also, that a close-range attack with explosives would likely produce more damage to himself than to those others—and that was even less comforting.

So how do you successfully attack a rolling, armored vehicle which is harder than anything you have to throw at it?

The answer to that was both obvious and simple.

In such a situation, you do not attack the vehicle. You attack, instead, those human systems inside it. Machines do not think and react on their own. Men do.

So he was going for the men, not the machine, as he formulated the plan of attack. The windows of that dreadnought were treated with a substance which rendered them almost opaque from the outside view, so he could not see the enemy nor even count their numbers. He could see shadowy movement, nothing more. The gunport was obvious enough, though—the distinctive snout of the Uzi warning enough—but there was a weakness, there, a limitation designed into a vehicle built for defense, not offense—the Maginot reasoning: impregnability at the expense of mobility. He knew the Uzi well—knew its firing characteristics, weight, length, feed. And he perceived in that gunport a limitation in the lines of fire available from such a weapon. Except for a few arc-degrees of horizontal mo-

49

bility, the Uzi would operate almost as a fixed weapon. Even so, it would provide a formidable gauntlet and a challenging test of Bolan's driving skills.

But it was possible to beat the Uzi.

The chief consideration remaining was that of terrain hospitability. He needed lateral displacement—at least twenty yards of it—and he needed a fast track in the breakaway. He found both, at a point where the roadway bent back westward near the edge of the lake, the terrain sloping away gently easterly on firm ground to the water's edge. This point probably represented the "now or never" of the attack plan—and Bolan went for it.

He floorboarded the eager Ferrari, leapt past the rear bumper of the sedately cruising limousine, and peeled away at a sharp angle along the sloping terrain as the Uzi erupted and raked him in a rising pattern of fire which began its impact just behind the right front wheel, sliced across the hood, and climbed immediately to the roof line.

So far, then, so good—without even a scratch.

The '79 was loaded and ready, extending a few inches beyond the right door, as he twirled the wheel hard right and slid into a bisecting course to rejoin the roadway.

The timing was perfect, the moment correct, and the fates smiling. He rejoined at about 100 feet above the approaching limousine which now was burning rubber in fast pursuit, fired his round, and plunged on across the roadway to a rocking halt just short of a dense stand of trees.

There had been no thought that a 40mm round of HE would actually breach the defenses of that Broadway tank. Such had not been the design of the attack. He was going for the human systems, not the engineering design of the machine. And apparently he'd found them. The HE impacted on the impregnable windshield directly in front of the driver seat, blew its fire in a trumpeting halo all about the forward compartment of that hurtling vehicle, and reached the reactive minds if not the flesh of the human components within.

The limousine staggered abruptly, heeled right, and plunged into the trees at the side of the road, tried and failed to climb an old one, caromed off in a backward fling, wedged itself driver's-side-down between two others.

Bolan was already clear of his own vehicle and feeding another round of HE into the '79. He sent it on ahead, this time with maximum effect. The armored hood to the engine compartment had sprung open, also a rear door. The HE impacted directly on target to lay another wreath of fire around the now vulnerable vehicle. It shuddered briefly, then gasoline vapors inside the engine compartment ignited.

Bolan closed immediately, but warily, circling for the best firing line into that blackened doorway.

But the time for caution was past.

He counted four bodies in there, clothing smouldering on two in the rear, broken heads and bloody renderings mutely crying the fate of the two in front.

There should have been six, in there.

He threw a glance along the backtrack, pursed his lips in silent thought, then clipped the '79 to his leg, closed the raincoat on it, and set off on foot, toward Central Park West.

It was probably going to be a damned long day.

CHAPTER 7

PRIORITIES

The big cop stood with both hands thrust deeply into his pants pocket and scowled into the wind, a faraway look in his eyes, as technicians carefully poked at the ruins of the armored vehicle and recorded the evidence. "Don't care how you try to reconstruct it," he growled to his undesired companion. "The facts remain the facts. Anyone with good eyes and police experience could tell you what happened here. The Ferrari overtook the Cadillac. He waited his chance, then went around at the bend in the road, cutting cross-country on wet grass, and he took seventeen slugs in the process. But he got ahead of them and he came back across, hell for leather. He fired a grenade right into their windshield. It didn't penetrate but it must have been a hell of a thing to see and experience, right into the face that way. The driver of the Cadillac simply lost control of his vehicle. The grenade didn't do it, except indirectly. The second grenade did not come until the Cadillac was lying on its side, right here, and this hard car had suddenly become very soft. Whatever the attempted reasoning, the intent at that point was purely aggressive and for no other reason than to seal the kill."

"It reads just as well the other way," insisted the U.S. marshal, "and it's a hell of a lot more believable. Whoever was driving the Ferrari could not also have been hurling bombs out the window at the same moment that he was fighting to control his vehicle. At the best, you have to allow two men in the Ferrari. Even at that, it's utterly ridiculous to suppose that one or two men in a car like that would deliberately take on an armored vehicle with six heavily armed torpedoes aboard. You say yourself that Minotti left the scene of the fire in a hell of a lather. Let's say that they pursued and overtook the Ferrari. Somehow they managed to maneuver him to the left side of the roadway and succeeded in running him completely off the road. His car was shot up and out of control on the wet grass. The Cadillac breezed on by, thinking their attack a success and now intent on putting the scene behind them. Enter, now, the unknown element. Maybe they were cruising back the other way, northbound. Or maybe they were just standing down here in the trees, waiting for them. Minotti and the other missing man, maybe. You tell me why these punks knock one another off, Captain, I don't understand it. But we all know they do."

"So where's the guy from the Ferrari?"

The marshal grinned solemnly. "Where's Minotti and the sixth man?"

"I wish I knew. But I can tell you this much. Your reasoning is inconsistent with the known facts. In the first place, nobody was 'hurling bombs.' We've got three witnesses that saw the man leave the burning building with a 'strange gun' in his hand. From the description, I'd call it an M-79 with a modified stock. That's a grenade launcher, pal. And that spells Mack Bolan in my book, every time. So does the rest of it. We can place the same individual leaving the scene of the fire in a red foreign sports car. That was fully twenty minutes before Minotti and his crew even showed up there. So who pursued whom from the scene? I call it a classic Bolan hit, and you know it's true. So why all the flak?"

The marshal grinned and lit a cigarette, gazed along the park road for a moment, then replied, "For the press, Captain? A matter of priorities?"

The orgcrime cop made a noise with his lips and stared at his feet. Then he displayed a brief, sober smile and said, "Okay, for the press, it looks like a gangland slaying. But we are pursuing other leads. Close enough?"

"Sounds reasonable," agreed the marshal.

"Tell Brognola he owes me one. Tell him, also, that I will never forget a rainy morning in Queens when I thought my town was getting respectable. Tell him I've not given up hope."

"Thanks, Cap'n. I'll deliver the messages." The marshal touched the brim of his hat and trudged away.

The cop called after him, "But tell 'im to put a rein on that guy. No more of this combat in the park bullshit."

The marshal did a walking pivot to toss off another relaxed salute. He went on down the road, climbed into an official U.S. government limousine, and settled with a sigh beside his chief.

"They'll cooperate," he reported.

"Good," said Brognola.

"What happened in Queens one rainy morning?"

"We buried Augie Marinello."

"Oh, that."

"Yeah. Following the wildest goddam slugfest this old city has ever seen. That was Striker's last visit."

"Rafferty wants you to curb him. No more public battles."

Brognola slid stiffly to the edge of the seat, hands clasped at his knees. "That's really rich, isn't it," he replied soberly. "Wish I had the control over that guy all these cops seem to think I have. I'd pull him out of here in a twink."

"A twink?" the marshal responded, grinning.

"Whatever. There's nothing here worth his little finger. And look at the way he flings himself around. You saw the goddam Ferrari. Shot to hell. And he still hasn't reported in." He called forward to the driver. "Check the battleship again, George."

The driver picked up a microphone and spoke into it.

The marshal reminded Brognola, "None of his blood back there, Chief. The way it reads to me, Minotti slipped away—either before or during the battle. I would guess that Striker is in hot pursuit."

"On foot?"

The marshal smiled. "Pole-vaulting on his dick, if that's the only way available. Tell you, I'd hate to have that guy on my trail. I would—"

He interrupted himself to listen to the radio exchange, up front. A pretty female voice was responding to the call from the chief.

"Babysitter."

From George: "Is he in?"

"Coming in now, via radio. What's your request?"

Brognola snatched up the remote mike and replied for himself. "Personal status report, please."

From April Rose: "A-OK, subject is clean. Stand by."

Brognola sighed and shot a triumphant look toward his task force leader. "A-OK," he repeated soberly.

"Told you," said the marshal, grinning.

The head fed quickly lit a cigar and settled into the cushions.

A moment later, April's perky voice reported: "Subject requests identical replacement vehicle. Requests that it be left in parking garage at target central, keys behind license plate."

"Tell him it's done," Brognola replied. Then he turned to the marshal and growled, "Christ, we've got to find another damned red Ferrari, and fast. Get on that, Dave, will you?"

"Sure." The marshal stepped outside, then stuck his head back into the car to ask, "Who pays for all this stuff?"

"He does."

"Where the hell does he get it?"

"He collects it from the boys."

"Really?"

"Sure. How poetic can you get? He makes them finance their own destruction."

The marshal chuckled, closed the door, and went on to his own vehicle.

Brognola called forward, "Let's go, George. Just cruise the park, for now."

The vehicle got underway, then April returned to the airwaves.

"Marco Polo got away."

Brognola replied, "So what is next?"

"Target central."

The chief groaned. "Is that really necessary?"

"He thinks so. Requests, also, info on female factor."

Brognola chomped on the cigar and gazed at the park scenery as he responded to that request. "No I.D., as yet, on the female factor. Condition guarded, prognosis unsure. Request subject supply amplifying data this regard."

April was obviously acting as a radio link between Brognola and Bolan. She came back after a brief pause with: "Sorry, no amplifying data available. Request maintain soft touch, priority handling. Subject is pursuing question of amplifying data. Requests diagnosis."

He replied, "Suspected narcotic shock of unknown origin. Tests underway to determine exact cause and treatment required. Prognosis uncertain, repeat, uncertain."

"Roger." A moment later, then: "That's all."

"Great," Brognola growled beneath his breath as he hung up the microphone. He told his driver, "Let's go back to the bus."

But it was not great. It was lousy as hell. New York did not need Mack Bolan. Certainly a nameless underage hooker, OD'd on God knew what, did not need him.

Washington, dammit—Washington needed him.

CHAPTER 8

THE BUY

If time could be bottled, somehow, and sold in a supermarket, its value would be difficult to determine. There were those "times" when ten minutes would slip by totally unnoticed, without apparent value, accomplishing nothing, meaning nothing. Other ten-minute stretches could be agonizing, ponderous, portentous, or tantalizing. Ten minutes with one's hand held over a flame could seem a lifetime. Ten minutes worth of sexplay would be, to most, too little. On the other hand, a ten-minute orgasm could kill.

Time, as Einstein noted, is always relative to

the event, the fourth dimension of the physical reality.

And so with warfare.

Only ten unbelievably telescoped minutes had elapsed since Bolan ventured into Central Park on Marco Minotti's tail. Emergency vehicles remained positioned outside Roman Nights. A few uniformed cops still wandered through the scene. Passersby on the park side continued to dawdle in small clumps—and Lou Nola still sat in a forlorn lump on a bench directly opposite his former place of employment.

Bolan sat down beside the little man, nudged him with an elbow, and quietly said, "Cheer up, sport. The best is yet to come."

Nola did a double take on the impressive figure beside him, stiffened, opened his mouth, closed it, then sank back into the defeated slump. After a moment of strained silence, he muttered, "What the hell is going on here?"

Bolan said, "That's what you're going to tell me, sport."

"That's funny, that's really funny." Nola said it bitterly, almost defiantly. "I've been ordered around, pushed around, slapped around, kicked around. For a lousy three hundred a week."

"Plus all you can steal," Bolan reminded him. "Don't forget the incentives."

"Incentives bullshit," Nola growled. "Marco says you're a counterfeit. Are you?"

"What do you say?" Bolan replied.

"I say I don't give a shit."

Bolan produced a sheaf of bills from an inside pocket, counted off ten one-hundreds as Nola watched curiously, placed the thousand in the little guy's hand.

"What's this for?"

"Incentive."

"I don't get you."

"I told you," Bolan reminded him, "that the best is yet to come. I like the way you handled yourself, in there. And with Marco. I saw it all. I liked what I saw."

Nola was beginning to thaw. "Yeah?"

"Yeah. Can we talk like men?"

"I hope so, sure." Nola put the money away and turned solemn eyes onto whoever the hell this guy was.

Bolan told him, "Marco is on a sinking ship and he knows it. That's why he acts like such a jerk."

Nola sniffed, "He's always acted that way, far as I'm concerned."

"But lately it has been worse," Bolan suggested.

"Maybe so. Maybe you're right. I never saw such a psycho bastard in all my life before. That son of a bitch is asking to get killed."

Bolan simply replied, "That's right."

"One of these days, someone is going to do it for him."

"You're right."

"I'd do it myself." Nola snapped his fingers. "Like that."

Bolan lit a cigarette, offered it to his companion, lit another, then said: "So do it."

"Is that what the grand is for?"

"Course not. The grand is my way of apologizing to a brother. I had to set you up. I caused you pain. I'm just telling you that I'm sorry about that."

Nola shrugged. "I'm not bleeding anywhere. What's the money really for?"

Bolan smiled at him. "It's an advance."

"Against what?"

"Don't you know when you're being recruited, guy?"

"Recruited for what?"

Bolan produced a note pad, scribbled an address, tore out the sheet and gave it to Nola. "Recognize the address?"

"No, I guess not."

"That's the headshed. You know what. Ever been there?"

"Me? I'm not even made. Three lousy bills a week."

Bolan quietly reminded him, "Now you've got ten. I am called Omega. You'll find me in the penthouse, or you can leave word."

The little man was definitely hooked now. "For what?"

"For whatever," Bolan replied, winking.

Nola was smiling that hideous smile, staring at the sheet of note paper. "You really are for real, then, aren't you?"

64

For reply, Bolan told him, "I make you Lou the Sport."

Which was a highly significant statement. In effect, Lou the Sport was now a "made" man.

He tried very hard to look solemn as he replied to that. "I guess I know what you want. I can tell you this much, already. She's been here the past three days. Marco brought her in late Wednesday night. Got me out of bed to come down here and tuck her away. Didn't trust the night people. Wrong blood. Anyway, that was the night he got back from New Mexico. He was in a hell of a sweat."

"She been like that the whole time?"

"Pretty much, yeah. Started puking yesterday. I didn't know what the hell to do. I could hardly stand to go in there. I only did about twice the whole time. Hell, it wasn't my responsibility. Didn't want her here. Who needs all that? For three bills a week? Who knows what the rap could be? Marco told me nothing, just to keep my damn mouth shut. This other guy came in three or four times a day, this Jew guy, used to be a doctor, I guess—he came in with his little bag three or four times a day, I guess. They're keeping her salted with something, I dunno what and I dunno why. None of my business, see. But I know that Marco was madder'n hell that you snatched her. Just who is that kid, anyway?"

"That's what I want you to find out for me, Sport."

Nola shrugged and replied, "Okay, I'll try. I don't know how the hell—"

"Do you have a quiet number for Marco?"

"Yeah."

"Wait about twenty minutes. Then call the quiet number. Tell him you suddenly remember something. Last time the doc came to see the kid, he left here in a red sports car. Someone picked him up, see, someone driving this red sports car. You know?"

Nola displayed the awful smile as he replied, "Yeah. I know exactly. You're something of a bastard, aren't you?"

Bolan smiled back and said, "I try to be, with scum like Marco trying to take over. After you make the call, you might try checking around, see what you can find out about the kid. Maybe something will come to mind, you'll remember something to tie her to. If you do, look for me at the penthouse. Otherwise, lay low and keep quiet. Uh, here's a guy can take messages for me." He whipped out the notepad, printed *Leo Turrin*, gave it to Nola. "Nobody else, just this guy."

"Okay."

The little man was looking troubled. Bolan asked him, "What's on your mind?"

Nola shrugged and replied, "I was just wondering how dangerous all this is."

Bolan told him, "Dangerous as hell, Sport."

"I thought so."

"You're a lot safer than Marco is, though."

66

"Yeah?"

"Yeah. Did you hear the rumpus over inside the park, few minutes ago?"

"Yeah. What was that?"

Bolan got to his feet. "Watch the noon news," he suggested casually. "Maybe you'll find out."

He went away from there then, without a backward glance, walking south with eyes alert for a taxicab.

Maybe that had been for nothing, back there. Then again, maybe not. A worm can always turn. Bolan was offering that one at least an opportunity to do so.

And he was onto something, for damn sure, he knew that. His combat shivers told him that it was so. He had found it highly interesting that Minotti's first known association with the kid came in the wake of his miserable disaster at White Sands.

But it was time, now, to try the penthouse—home of the Aces.

He would decide, later, just how valuable had been the two-minute bottle of time he'd purchased from Lou the Sport.

CHAPTER 9

ACES HIGH

It was a 28-floor modern building in the heart of the high rent district, once among the proudest possessions of the Marinello group. During his heydey, Augie had signed over the top three floors to be used as the "corporate offices" for *La Cosa Nostra,* via a longterm, dollar-a-year lease.

It was not so magnanimous a gift as one would be led to believe. Augie had muscled his way into the legitimate company which was bankrolling construction of the building, bankrupted it via control over the labor that was building it and the city departments who certified the work, and emerged as sole owner after paying off twelve cents on the dollar to the bankruptcy receiver who himself belonged to the Marinello group. And although *La Cosa Nostra,* "This Thing of Ours," was billed as a sort of United Nations for international crime, Augie had always had the Thing in his pocket, as well.

The net effect of all that was that the Boss of Bosses had stolen a multi-million dollar building, then took statesman honors (plus a nice tax write-off) by deeding three floors to a tax-exempt corporation which he, in effect, also owned.

In the long look, though, Augie had indeed done the brothers a favor. The building itself had been seized by the IRS when Augie's star began to fall, as were all the other legitimate holdings which could be legally tied to the Marinello estate, at his death. That estate would be cast in concrete for years to come, so involved were its many convolutions through the business community. But the longterm lease to the "Foundation for American Unity" was legally binding and untouchable—at least so long as that "foundation" continued to exist.

Bolan was here to see that it ceased to exist, as of today.

He had already driven in the toppling wedge, on his earlier visit to this complicated old city. *La Commissione,* or the Council of Bosses, had once been an effective and effcient administrative group which saw to the management of the worldwide networks of organized crime. It was, after all, a business; crime does not "organize" without an organizational technique; in its heyday, *La Commissione* could have taught the legitimate conglomerates and cartels a thing or two about high finance and manipulative management. It appears, in fact, that they did so.

But *La Commissione* existed both in the particular and in the abstract. The *particular* body consisted of a small army of hoodlums, wheeler-dealers, and legal eagles who actually saw to the day-to-day details of corporate management. The *abstract* body were the bosses themselves, a motley assortment of jungle lords who had risen through blood and plunder to absolute rule over the various crime territories comprising the North American continent. The abstract body did not sit in daily congress at the top of Augie's building. Those guys rarely saw one another, largely did not even like one another, certainly did not trust one another.

The origin of the "aces" is clouded in myth and legend, but the need for such a group could be inferred from the most elemental understanding of *La Commissione* and its two bodies, the particular and the abstract.

It seems likely that, in the beginning, an "Ace" was a physical stand-in for a family ruler at the Council of Bosses—part overseer, part diplomat, part businessman, part enforcer. It must have been an interesting job, in such a congress of thieves. But it probably worked out rather well, in the beginning. Too well, perhaps. As the crime families grew fat and their territories fatter, complications arose. Each Ace began to see the need for administrative assistants, those assistants soon began to need assistants—and a bureaucracy arose.

At the height of American Mafia influence, more than two hundred "administrators" toiled daily for the "foundation." By that time, the role of the aces themselves had undergone a dramatic transformation. They now constituted an elite gestapo force, atop a world of their own making—exclusively occupying the 28th floor or "penthouse," their staffs flowing from wall to wall across the 26th and 27th floors of the building.

The aces controlled the whole glorious "Thing." And there were pyramids of power in that penthouse, beginning at the top with the Aces of Spades, then the clubs, followed by the lower echelon "red aces"—hearts and diamonds —but aces all, virtually autonomous and serving now no particular boss or family but the "Thing" itself, *La Cosa Nostra*.

This, then, was for all practical purposes *La Commissione*. It is said—and now generally believed to be true—that Marinello himself, with his silent partner, Barney Matilda, was the mastermind and secret guiding force behind the modern council. It is certainly true that it was Marinello's inspiration which installed the aces as a veritable *gestapo* with the power of life and death within the organization.

Bolan had changed all that.

Marinello was now dead. Barney Matilda was dead. All the old bosses were dead. All the territories were wobbly, disorganized, out of hand —and new ethnic groups were moving into the vacuum, setting up their own. Political clout routes were now unreliable, shifting, disappearing. Organized labor was beginning to police itself. Legitimate covers were shredded, exposed, toppling. The assets of hundreds of corporate structures around the country were now under IRS seal, the Securities and Exchange Commission was investigating scores more, and the vast wealth of an invisible empire was quickly grinding down to nought.

In effect, *La Commissione* itself was dead.

La Cosa Nostra was becoming a thing of the past, a clouded historical footnote to America's 20th century.

And, in the same fell swoop which brought it all about, Bolan had made it appear that the aces themselves were largely responsible for the fall.

It was not now an easy time for those guys, those that were left to view the disaster.

Some of them had departed the country. Others, with less to fear from outraged survivors, had gone into quiet and anonymous retirement in various regions of the sunbelt. Those with the courage or prestige to remain did not venture far from the atmospheres of New York City and even then walked very softly.

73

There was, of course, a vestige of empire to be maintained. But the 26th and 27th floors were much quieter, these days. A skeleton force took care of routine diplomatic chores and tried to maintain communications between remnants of the empire.

Leo Turrin had emerged as the power beneath the penthouse.

According to Turrin, the penthouse itself was virtually a deserted sanctum, manned routinely by a couple of red aces and visited occasionally by an Ace of Clubs called *Sigmund.*

As reported also by Turrin, an Ace of Spades identified as *Frankie* was the only one thought to be still operating across the various territories. And, of course, like Omega, Frankie was Mack Bolan.

So Frankie/Omega was coming home.

He was coming to reclaim his own.

Let the legless bosses beware.

CHAPTER 10

TARGET CENTRAL

The express elevator served the top three floors only, from either the garage level or the main lobby. Bolan boarded in the lobby and went directly to the penthouse. The elevator opened onto a small foyer, beyond which and behind closed glass doors lay an expansive, open room with glass at three sides and a wraparound, open-air terrace. The fourth side of that top floor, the elevator side, was given over to private offices, one of which Bolan had taken to himself during his *command strike*, some time earlier. That had been a time of utter confusion for the mob, though; a successful penetration might not be so easy, this time.

He took a key from his wallet, tried it in the lock at the heavy glass doors, turned it, and stepped inside. So okay. They had not even changed the damned locks.

Just inside stood a massive, horseshoe-shaped desk which had served, in better times, as a reception desk for visiting VIPs. Nothing was stirring in that big room, now. It was immaculately clean, though, smelled faintly of Lysol spray, and sounded good via faint background music issuing from concealed speakers.

Well, after all, it was a Saturday morning. How many "corporate offices" in this city would be bursting with activity at such a time?

Bolan went on past the reception area and headed straight toward Omega's office, the larger and central of three luxurious enclosures at the back wall. Beyond there would be a labyrinth of small offices, conference rooms, two kitchens and a wine "cellar."

His hand was on the door and he was about to step inside the office when a handsome young man appeared in the doorway to his left. Bolan had never seen this guy before, but he knew what he was.

"Sir? Can I help you?" the minor ace inquired politely.

"Not right now," Bolan replied brusquely. "I will let you know."

"Shouldn't we observe the formalities? May I have your marker?"

Bolan frowned, dug out his ID wallet, handed it to the guy.

The ace smiled and stepped back into his office.

Bolan went on into his "own" office, removed his hat and coat, took off the M-79 rig and hung it beneath the coat, went to his desk.

He had hardly settled into the chair when a connecting door opened and the younger man joined him. These guys were nobody's damned fools, minor or not. All of them had been college educated, were impeccable in both dress and manners, had minds like springtraps. They were the underworld equivalent of the CIA— and, no, there was not a fool among them.

The guy returned the ID wallet and said, "Welcome home, sir. We've missed you."

Which was a baldfaced lie.

Bolan growled, "What is this place? Death warmed over? Where is everyone?"

The guy spread his hands and calmly replied, "Well, it's Saturday."

"Tell it to Marco," Bolan snapped. He held out his hand. "But first let's see yours."

It took the guy aback, a bit. But he smiled, produced the marker, and took a seat beside the desk.

Bolan placed the card on the desk and turned the face up. Uh huh, the guy was a Diamond. The counterfeit Spade removed a small key from a magnetic hook on the underside of the desk, opened the center drawer where he found another key which opened the "safe" lower-right drawer. In there was the metal box which was supposed to be there, and in the metal box was a small leatherbound notebook which contained all the "keys" to this kingdom.

Bolan had one precisely like it in the War-wagon.

But he was playing for effect, now, and he wanted it to look good. He found the guy's number on the tenth page. The reds did not have enough rank to deserve code names. This one was listed as Donald Rutiglio.

Bolan closed the book, returned it to the box, put the box away, slid the card across to the guy, put a foot on the edge of the desk, clasped his hands behind his head, and said, "We've never met."

"No, sir. I've been at home office only since, uh . . ."

Bolan said the unsayable. "Since things went to hell. It's okay to say it. But it's not okay for it to stay that way. I'm going to ask you again. Where is everyone? Where the hell, especially, is Sigmund?"

Rutiglio shifted about in his chair for a moment, as though seeking some diplomatic angle, then replied, "We don't see much of Sigmund. To be perfectly candid, sir, you hit it right on the head. This place is, in fact, death warmed over."

Bolan put his foot down, lit a cigarette, blew smoke at the guy as he told him: "Not for long. Vacation's over, Donald. Call Leo the Pussy up here. I want him here in two minutes flat. And he'd better be here, Saturday or not."

Rutiglio smiled and got to his feet as he replied, "They don't call him that now, sir. Mr. Turrin practically runs the place now. I'm sure he's around but he's very seldom at his desk. Good man. I'll run down and find him."

"Do that," Bolan growled.

The guy smiled and went out.

Cool. Minor or not, the guy was cool as death. These were the Mafiosi, Bolan knew, who had inspired novelists and filmmakers for decades to produce those portraits of invincible Mafia hitmen who were all cold purpose and unswerving dedication. They were, thank God, a decided minority within Mafia ranks. Most of the "boys," while vicious as hell, certainly, were not all that efficient, were ruled by vanity and greed, were given to destructive emotions, were unreliable, untrustworthy, and largely unworthy.

These guys were something else; and, yes, Bolan was damned glad that most of them were gone. So long as even one remained near the thrones of power, savages like Marco Minotti could make it big again, and spread their savage greed to the four corners of the world again.

Dammit, it would not happen. It would not.

He pulled up the left leg of his trousers and removed an oblong box which was held there by rubber bands. It was roughly the size and shape of a ten-pack carton of regular cigarettes. It was not a carton of cigarettes but a radio transceiver engineered to the highest state of the art. He extended the small, telescoping antenna and carried it out through the lounge area to the terrace.

Twenty seconds later, he'd found the optimum location for it, peeled away protective paper from the "death grip" adhesive on the backside, emplaced it, and activated it.

A relay in the Warwagon's intelligence banks would now be open to receive transmissions from that radio source. But it was also a receiver of transmissions—in fact, a multi-receiver operating simultaneously on six different pickup frequencies—and it was a recorder, as well, with impulse-actuated relays and six recording channels.

Those six channels would be fed by microminiature "bugs" which were small enough to be concealed within a telephone transmitter. All that was left, now, was to get the bugs emplaced.

He placed one in his own telephone, one in each of the other offices, one at the horseshoe desk, and saved two for Turrin.

Then he checked his Beretta, installed the silencer, placed it on his desk beneath a manila folder, and got ready to receive his guests.

He expected some, yeah.

He expected most anybody . . . and anything.

CHAPTER 11

GETTING TOGETHER

April Rose was busy at the console when Brognola stepped aboard the cruiser. She was a tall girl, strikingly constructed with nice hips and breasts, commanding eyes and shoulder-length dark hair—who would have thought, Brognola wondered, that she'd graduated at the top of her engineering class, picked up graduate honors in solid-state physics—and then, of all things, sought a career in government service. Cloak and dagger damned service, at that.

She would look a lot more at home as an NFL cheerleader or draped across the center-fold of *Playboy*.

The subject of his ruminations flashed a smile

at her boss and murmured, "A minute, please."

He went to the con, sat down, lit a cigar and watched the girl at her work. Damned good at it, yeah. Brognola felt a bit guilty, though. This had not been the plan. The girl had been a total neophyte in field work. To make her first assignment . . . Dammit, he'd not meant to involve her to this extent. Her own damned fault, of course. He'd warned her. He'd warned her about Bolan. "You'll probably fall for the guy," he'd told her. "Most women do. Not that he's a lover boy, or anything like that. Quite the opposite. There's just one thing on that guy's mind, and it's not love. So remember that. And keep your distance. Unless you want a lot of pain. He's a walking dead man."

She'd flashed those luminous eyes and replied, "Don't worry about me, chief. Mr. Bolan does not sound like my cup of tea, anyway."

Hah!

He had given her the full briefing, of course. Told her things about the man and his war such as he'd told no one else, ever. He'd considered it necessary—as much for her benefit as his. And he'd seen the disapproval in her eyes. No, she had not liked the man.

Until she met him, in the flesh.

Six days ago. Could that be possible?—six lousy days ago?

She was hooked, now, that was so obvious.

Ah well . . .

April looked up from the console with a

twisted little smile, as though she'd picked up some of the vibes of Brognola's thoughts. But she said, "It seems to be going great."

"What's happening?"

She tossed her pretty head to get rid of a troublesome lock of hair and replied, "Not much, yet. Our man just walked in and took the place over. I'll never be able to understand how he does that."

"Sheer guts," Brognola growled. "Is it wired?"

"Six channels, yes."

"Can I listen in?"

She shook the question away, explaining: "Not live. Doesn't work that way. The black box receives and stores each individual channel on a ten-minute program. At the termination of each program, it dumps to the computer, all six tracks at once. Time requirement for the dump is ten seconds. During those ten seconds, inputs via the receiver are assembled on a storage buffer—that is, held in a delay circuit—then printed over to tape when the dump is completed. So the data collection causes no gaps between record programs."

"So how do I find out what's going on up there?"

"I've been setting it up for you," she replied, smiling. "Look at your terminal."

Brognola swivelled his head toward the forward computer. The monitor was illuminated and displaying "Audio Program."

"Your controls are the numerals 1 through 6,"

April explained. "Those numerals correspond to the individual recording tracks. Striker is on Channel One. Sticker is Channel Four. I do not know the precise locations of the other four pickups."

"I just punch the numeral 1 and enter?" he said.

"Right. That will put you on Striker, beginning with the first dump. Punch 'one point one' for the next dump, 'one point two' for the second, and so on. The computer has already eliminated null periods so that the conversations will appear continuous even if there are long gaps between data. But you do have the ten-minute frame of reference."

Brognola growled, "Right," and leaned over the terminal.

"By the way," April said, "who is Sigmund?"

"What about Sigmund?"

"He walked into Striker's office just prior to the latest dump. All I have so far are their greetings."

Brognola sighed, rotated his shoulders, and punched the numeral one on his keyboard.

The guy rapped lightly on the door and walked on in without an invitation to enter. Medium height, athletic build, strong face, hard eyes, deceptively relaxed manner—age, anyone's guess—somewhere between thirty and sixty. Bolan had never seen this one, either, but he knew immediately who he was.

"How's it swinging, Sigmund?" he inquired casually.

The Ace of Clubs went straight to the window, gazed outside for a moment, turned back with a thin smile, said: "It's not swinging at all, I'm afraid. The pendulum has stopped, sir."

"The slightest touch will start it again," Bolan told him.

The guy turned back to the window. He lit a cigarette, took a deep pull at it, exhaled noisily, put both hands in his pockets, swivelled his head to look at the man behind the desk. "Is that why you're here?"

Bolan sent him a hard look as he replied, "I'm here because I'm here."

"Sorry, I didn't mean . . ." Sigmund took another hard pull at the cigarette. "I was in Europe when, uh . . ."

"You were in Zurich."

A small light flared in those eyes. "You know me better than I know you, sir."

"Shouldn't I?"

Sigmund smiled, went to the desk, put out the cigarette, leaned forward to visually scan Bolan's face and hands. "May I get personal?"

Bolan smiled. "Why not?"

"I like your face. Who did it?"

A small item of shoptalk. But Bolan smiled on and replied, "That's too personal."

And so it was. If the legends had any basis in fact, these guys changed faces almost as casually as they changed suits. A quiet penthouse joke for years was to the effect that the clubs and spades sometimes forgot who they really were. The idea, of course, was to induce others to forget.

In fact, Bolan's present face was not the one he'd started the war with. A close look at the proper areas would reveal the telltale marks of "facial restructuring."

Sigmund said, "You're right, it is. Especially now. To put it right up front, sir, I'm a little surprised that you are here."

"Why?"

"Well, I just—you were here when it went to hell, weren't you?"

Bolan said, coldly, "I was."

"So there's a lot of hate in this town."

"There's hate everywhere," Bolan reminded the ace.

"Especially here, though."

Bolan shrugged. "I thrive on it. But they don't hate me, Sigmund. They hate what their Thing has become. We're going to change it."

"Just the two of us? Because that's all that's left, you know. Sometimes I wonder if it isn't better this way." The ace sighed and dropped into a chair opposite the desk. "What's left, you know, isn't really worth the effort. Unless . . ."

"Unless what?" Bolan growled.

"Unless we can get this guy Bolan. He's back in town, too."

88

The guy put a bit too much emphasis on the "too."

"Have you seen him?" Bolan inquired softly.

"Who ever sees him? But he's here. He is. I have spent all my time since the return from Europe studying the guy, doping him, trying to figure him. I think I know, now, how he operates, how he does it."

"That's interesting," Bolan replied. "I've been doing the same thing. In the field, though."

"Yes, I uh, I understand that you've been quite active, Omega. Are you also Frankie?"

"I'm a lot of people," Bolan said coldly. "Don't try to spot me, Sigmund. It's been tried by the best. Including Barney, also known as Peter, also known as The Rock, etcetera, etcetera."

Sigmund's manner underwent a total transformation. He seemed to relax, thaw. "Barney was the rock upon which the church was built." He lit another cigarette. "I thought I was the only one who knew that."

"Did you know," Bolan asked quietly, confidingly, "that the Talifero brothers were Barney's kids? I mean, for real flesh and blood."

The guy's chin dropped. He flicked the ash from his cigarette and said, "That's—is that gospel?"

"It's gospel," Bolan quietly assured the guy. "He told me about it just before he died. Just before . . ." He swept the room with his hand. "Just before he left me this."

"I knew," Sigmund commented in a hushed voice, "that this office was the seat of power. But it was never occupied, never a soul here. I used to come in and just sit at the desk, sometimes. Feels good, doesn't it. I spotted old Barney coming out of here one night, though—oh, couple of years ago. He knew I'd spotted him, too. Which, I've always believed, is why I suddenly found myself with the European assignment."

"How is it over there?" Bolan inquired, changing the subject, he hoped.

"Bad enough. But not so bad as here. They've been pulling money from the numbered accounts like there was no bottom to the barrel. So the Taliferos were . . ."

"They lost forty or fifty mil yesterday," Bolan said.

"Yes, I heard. That makes about five hundred mil, just this past week or so. Between us brothers, Omega, there's not that much left to save. When Augie died . . ."

"There's more to it than money," Bolan pointed out, trying to keep the conversation centered on the here and now. "Money is a fluid. It flows this way and that. We can get it flowing right again if we can get the Thing right, again. And I think you're right—the guy Bolan is the key. What makes you think he's here?"

"I know he's here," said the Ace of Clubs.

"How?"

"He's hit Marco twice already this morning."

"How do you know it was Bolan?"

"It adds that way. I've been doing a lot of commuting to Washington the past couple of weeks. I have some sources there. I think I know what the guy is doing, and how. He's here, right now. I think he's here for the knockout punch."

"What knockout?" Bolan asked quietly.

"The whole thing. I believe he means it as his swan song."

"What does that mean?"

"I believe he's going in with the feds."

"How would you get something like that?"

"I told you, I have sources."

"But if the feds know what the guy is doing . . ."

"Exactly," Sigmund said with a smug smile.

"You think they're sponsoring him?"

"I think so, yes."

"For how long?"

Sigmund shrugged. "What does it matter? If they *are* sponsoring him *now* . . ."

Silence reigned over that office for a moment before Bolan said, "You'd better give me what you have."

"There have been massive federal movements all this past week," Sigmund reported, hunching conspiratorially closer. "There's a guy, Harold Brognola—he's a special assistant to the Attorney General. That's for the public view. Among those in the know, though, it is very quiet knowledge that this guy Brognola works directly out of the White House. Well, so, these movements—these federal movements are by some sort of hush-hush task force led by Brognola. Would you like to hear the itinerary?"

Bolan growled, "I can guess."

"Your guess is right," Sigmund replied, reading his face. "These are airlift operations involving several large government transports. They're carting around buses loaded with all sorts of sophisticated electronic gear. Plus a damned army of federal marshals. It can't be a coincidence that they turn up everywhere Bolan does."

"Not hardly," said Bolan himself.

"They're here today."

"You're sure of that?"

"The transports are parked out at Kennedy, right now."

"Maybe it's an all-out effort to catch the guy. He's one of the most-wanted men. Or, supposedly."

"Supposedly is right," said Sigmund. "It just doesn't read that way. I think they're supporting him."

"Well that's a hell of a note," Bolan growled.

"That's what I say. When the damned government starts coming down on the side of a guy like that . . ."

"It's scary," declared the "guy like that."

"Worse, yet," said Sigmund. "I'm afraid the guy is carrying one of our markers."

Bolan tried to look appropriately disturbed

by that bit of news. "Where do you get that?" he growled.

"Nothing for sure . . . but it does seem to read that way. I think maybe he's been carrying it for a long time. That could be why there's so much hate in the country. If you get me."

Omega got him, all right. Mack Bolan got him, too. Straight down the pike. This Ace of Clubs was dangerous as hell. He should have been a Spade. Maybe he would have become one except for the insane secrecy cloaking this nutty penthouse. If Barney had not sent the guy away . . .

"I guess it's just you'n me, now, pal," Bolan told that Club. "Let's see what we can put together."

Hal Brognola lifted a full twelve inches out of his chair and yelled, "Well Jesus Christ!"

"What is it?" April cried.

"Don't ask! Just don't ask!"

The chief was up and out of there in a twinkling, leaving April to puzzle the thing through for herself.

She set up the program in the master terminal, put on the headset, and pushed the proper button.

Minutes later she slumped wearily against the console, swiped angrily at a tear on the cheek, and whispered, "My God!"

Brognola's concern was perfectly understandable, of course, in view of the disconcerting counter-intelligence contained in Audio Program 1.2—the revelation of a dangerous leak in official Washington which could doom not only Bolan's New York strike but the Phoenix Project, as well.

But the chief's hasty departure had occurred moments before the collection of program 1.3—and the revelation there was even more frightening.

Marco Minotti and his "troops" had just arrived at Mafia headquarters.

At White Sands, just a few days ago, Bolan and Minotti had stood toe to toe and eyeball to eyeball—and Marco had lived to remember the encounter.

He was, April knew, perhaps the one Mafioso in New York who could blow Mack Bolan's cover.

Forever, yes. Forever.

CHAPTER 12

FULL HOUSE

Leo stuck his head in the door to announce, "Minotti and his troops are on the way up."

"How many?" Bolan-Omega inquired.

"Five carloads."

"Make them comfortable in the lounge," the Ace of Spades instructed. "We'll be with 'em in a minute."

Then he turned to Sigmund and asked him, "Did you know he was coming?"

The guy nodded his head and replied, "I called him."

"Why?"

"Seemed the thing to do." Sigmund spread

his hands in an explanatory gesture. "Face it, Marco's the boss, now."

Bolan growled, "The hell you say."

"*He* says it," replied Sigmund with a solemn smile.

"And you say it," Bolan growled.

"Okay, sure, I came down on the power side. To tell the truth, I was leaning toward Santelli until yesterday. But Tommy is gone, now. Marco is the only power left."

"Marco is a streetcorner hood."

"So was Augie, thirty years ago. So were they all. I can work with Marco. Can you?"

Bolan-Omega replied, "I'd rather not."

"Do you have a viable alternative?"

"I'd damn sure like to come up with one."

"Would you feel better, then," said Sigmund, "if I withhold the kiss for a while?"

"I'm telling you to do so," Bolan said quietly.

"Then I will, of course. But if I may advise you . . . our position here, now, is very tenuous. It seems that you and I are the only monitors left in the game. One unwise move and . . ."

"Have you been briefing Marco with regard to the Washington angle?"

"Only very sketchily," Sigmund replied. "Enough to gain his confidence." He smiled craftily. "*Not* enough to make my own services no longer required."

Bolan smiled back. "You should be a Spade."

"I think so, too, naturally."

"We'll make it official as soon as we get the new Thing structured."

"Thanks," Sigmund said, candidly adding: "It's long overdue."

"I recommended you two years ago," Bolan-Omega declared quietly, adding his own touch of candor to the conversation.

"Was that before or after . . . ?"

"Before," Bolan replied.

"Well, so, we both know what happened to that recommendation." The guy chuckled. "It went to Europe."

So the Ace of Clubs had a sense of humor. Even ironic humor. It was nice to know that. Bolan chuckled with him as he confided, "Mine went to South America twice before it finally got home."

They were buddies, now—confidants, in this wacky world of Mafia intrigue.

Sigmund got to his feet, cracked the door open, peered into the lounge, said, "They're here, I believe. Would you like for me to go out and . . ?"

Bolan quickly said, "Yeah, I wish you would. I'm not sure I can look that blowfish in the face."

Sigmund almost giggled. He straightened his face, said, "Well, I've had a lot of practice at it," and went on out.

Bolan sighed, retrieved his Beretta from beneath the manila folder, removed the silencer, restored the piece to the shoulder holster.

No. He damned sure did not want to face that guy. Not in this time and circumstance.

Leo Turrin was waiting for them at the elevator. He grabbed Minotti's hand and wrung it warmly as he exclaimed, "God, it's good to see you, Marco! I was worried—I heard about—hey, that hit in the park is all over the damned news! Who the hell . . ?"

Three of the boys went on ahead to scout the lounge area, two more took stations in the foyer, and the two personal tagmen fell in to the rear as Turrin walked Minotti inside.

A good guy, this Leo. Minotti liked him, respected him. He'd like to make this guy in his own image. But Leo Turrin was not the guy he'd come to see, right now. "Where's Sigmund?" he growled.

"Sit down, get comfortable," Turrin said. "Sigmund is in a parley with Omega. They'll be out in a minute. What are you drinking? Naw —I know." He turned to his boy at the bar and snapped his fingers. "Scotch and Perrier for Mr. Minotti."

It was kind of funny. Leo had been a ranker up north when Marco was still hustling dimes in the Bronx. Why he'd ever traded that for . . .

Minotti dropped into a heavy leather chair and said, "You run a tight ship, Leo. Don't know what we'd do without you up here. But any time you want to spring from this joint, you let me know."

Turrin grinned as he inquired, "You got something particular in mind?"

Minotti leaned forward to light a cigar. He relaxed into the chair, blew a perfect smoke ring, watched it rise toward the ceiling, said, "I got a lot in mind. We gotta get back to the basics. Too much time and money went legit. Now look where it's at. We need to put our money where the feds can't get at it. Back to the basics."

Turrin tossed a look toward the back wall, pulled up a chair in close conference, replied: "That's exactly what I've been thinking, myself, Marco."

"Yeah." It was Minotti's favorite topic, of late. "You just keep on thinking, Leo. The old outfit will rise again. And I like the way you handled the girls franchise, up north. That's what we need to concentrate on. That kind of stuff, you know. I already took my bath in the other kind. You know what I mean. Everything went to shit, too, didn't it. You can't compete in the legit marketplace nowadays. Shit, the goddam legit marketplace, now, is kinkier than we ever thought of. You can't compete with that, not with the feds always on your ass, too."

"I know what you mean," Turrin said, glowing at him.

"Sure you do. Because you're a sharp guy. You're a vanishing breed, though, Leo. Hell, in the old days . . . well, you know what I mean. Guys that couldn't dust my butt with a dollar bill are now operating most of the hard markets. Listen, we let it get out of hand. I mean to get it back. And if you want in . . ."

"You know I do," Turrin said quietly. "I've been like on vacation here at *commissione*. I'm walking the damned walls, I tell you. I'd die for a chance at another territory."

"I knew it," Minotti said. "Well, listen, the smart money today is in sex. S, E, X. And not just prostitution, you know. Hell, they said the sex revolution would kill prostitution. Don't you believe that. It's never been better. But we lost control of it. We can get it back. But that's just one angle. There's a whole new field opening up. You ever hear of video cassettes?"

Turrin said, "Sure. I've been looking at that, myself."

"Well, keep on looking." Minotti was playing politician, campaigning for votes. Promise them anything but just make sure you talk their own language. "It's going to be an exciting territory, a gold mine, for a savvy guy. You know why most people don't go to porno theatres? That's right, most don't, a small percentage do. You know why? Because most people are hypocrites. They'd all like to see the action, sure, but they don't want to be seen doing it. Offer it to them in their homes and they'll spend the family budget to get their private kicks. A real wiseguy could clean up in that market, Leo. You be thinking about it."

Turrin assured him, "I sure will, Marco."

"Where the hell is that Sigmund? Does he know I'm here?"

"He knows you're here, Marco. He's skulling the battle strategy right now with—"

"I should be part of that. What is that other guy called?"

"He's called Omega. You remember him. He saved my ass at Pittsfield."

Minotti pulled on a dark frown. "He's the one that blew the whistle on old Barney?"

"That's the one."

"That fuckin' Augie, Leo!"

"Yeh. If Omega hadn't come down on the right side, no telling what . . ."

"You're right, no telling what. Well I want to meet this guy Omega. I especially want to know where he was at this morning about eight o'clock or so."

"He was right here," Turrin said.

"Right here?"

"That's right. He was here at six when I came in."

"You come in at *six?*"

Turrin smiled. "Every morning, seven a week."

"Was Sigmund here?"

"At six? No."

"How 'bout eight?"

"No. He came in about half an hour ago."

"He called me about half an hour ago, too," Minotti muttered darkly. "Do you know what kind of car he drives?"

"A Mercedes," Turrin replied immediately. "SL something or other."

"How 'bout the other guy?"

Turrin shook his head. "I don't know. Whatever you're thinking, Marco, I say you should give Omega benefit of the doubt. He is—"

"I'm wondering about a damned red Ferrari and a guy who calls himself a Black Ace. The thing in the park? It was a set up. You wouldn't know anything about . . ."

Turrin solemnly replied, "Just what I heard on the news, Marco. Who set it up?"

"That's what I mean to find out," Minotti said, glowering with the memory of it.

"Well here comes Sigmund, now," Turrin observed. "You want me to stick around and listen in?"

Minotti turned a dark gaze toward the approaching Ace. "Naw," he replied quietly. "Leave us. And go tell this Omega that I want his ass at front and center, too. Wait, cancel that. I don't want them together. Tell Omega I'll be in to see him in a minute."

Another elevator car loaded with Minotti's boys had just arrived. They were spilling into the lounge like a war party, solemn of stride and with restless gaze.

Turrin smiled, stood up, and said, "I'm sure he's looking forward to seeing you, too, Marco."

Then he danced around Sigmund and struck off very quickly toward the offices at the back wall.

CHAPTER 13

SET UP

"He'll be coming in any minute," Turrin warned his friend, the Striker.

"Did you reach Grazzi?"

"Yes. It should take him another ten, fifteen minutes to get here, though. I doubt that we can stall it that long."

"Where's Billy Gino?"

"Garage level. Marco left a full crew down there. Billy's watching them. I told Grazzi to park on the street and use the main lobby."

Bolan went to the window and adjusted the blinds. "Okay, Leo. Thanks. Keep the fingers crossed. It's not lost, yet."

"Course not. Uh, maybe I should stay in here with you, though."

"No. Mix around, jolly it up all you can. Try to get some booze inside those people."

"I should alert Hal."

"No need to. I'm sure he's reading the wires. Just hope he doesn't come busting in and tear it for good. If you're reading me, Hal—don't! Wait a minute! Check that! Do it! But don't come for me! Come for Sigmund!"

Turrin marveled, "What the hell . . ?"

"Sigmund is in damned big trouble," Bolan said, grinning. "Someone had better come spring his butt out of here."

"You're right!" Turrin howled. "My God, it's beautiful. It's beautiful!"

They left the personnel bus double-parked on the street just outside the garage entrance and jogged down the ramp in combat order, two single files at double armreach apart, fifty United States marshals in crisp uniforms and bearing riot guns, Harold Brognola leading them by two paces.

A mob of torpedoes milling around outside the office to the underground garage offered no resistance but quickly parted ranks and allowed the formation to pass unobstructed. One file of marshals dropped away to take up scowling positions opposite the torpedoes while the other contingent jogged on to the elevators.

104

A guy whom Brognola recognized immediately as Billy Gino thrust his chin into Brognola's path and growled, "You got no right to go up there!"

"Do tell," said Brognola as he brushed the guy aside, but gently.

Brognola and ten took the express to the penthouse. Another ten took another car to the 27th. Five more ran up the stairway to neutralize the main lobby.

Leo Turrin met Brognola in the penthouse foyer, obviously alerted to the invasion by a lookout below. Two torpedoes stood behind him.

"You can't come in here without a warrant!" Turrin growled.

Brognola produced one, thrust it at his star undercover operative, and growled back, "Jam this up your ass and read it, then, hotshot!"

Turrin recognized the form of the warrant as one of many carried in the rolling command center, duly dated and executed by the special federal judge who traveled with them. He winked knowingly as Brognola and his force of ten pushed on past him.

Minotti stood just inside the lounge, scowling.

Turrin showed him a pained face and shrugging shoulders.

Minotti whirled about and retreated to the interior, several of his boys closing around him.

Sigmund sat in the same chair which Leo

had vacated some minutes earlier, thoughtfully puffing at a cigarette, seemingly bored by the whole thing.

The marshals formed a fanshaped pattern at the open doorway, weapons cradled across the chest, as Brognola penetrated into the lounge, alone. He halted ten paces away from Sigmund, gave him a hard look, and said, "Okay, pal, let's go."

Sigmund looked to his left and to his right, then at Brognola. "You talking to me?" he inquired casually.

"The game is over," Brognola snapped. "It's now or never." He raised a hand and pointed dramatically at Minotti. "Tell your dogs to lie down, Marco! I'd rather take this man out of here peacefully and quietly. But I'll do it any way I have to!"

Minotti sneered and turned away. "You're welcome to him," he said, over his shoulder.

Sigmund rose slowly to his feet, a frozen figure uncoiling into some nightmare, the face a twisted mask of protest. "Well now, wait a minute . . ."

Brognola moved close and quietly told that guy, "Suit yourself, Sigmund. I'll leave you here if you're sure that's really what you want. You're a dead bird either way, now, so it makes no difference to me. Stay, if you want to, and save the taxpayers some money."

"You cute bastard!" Sigmund hissed.

Minotti was watching closely from a distance, too far away to overhear the conversation.

Brognola shrugged, turned his back on Sigmund, walked swiftly toward the exit.

Sigmund briefly scanned that room, read the scowling faces there, then quickly followed.

Brognola waited for him at the door, then took him arm in arm to the elevator—the marshals backing away in a protective shield to the rear.

As the doors were closing on that little charade, Leo Turrin yelled from the lounge, "You're a dead man, Sigmund!"

Brognola grinned, offered a cigar to his prize patsy, and said, "You just saved the day, pal."

Maybe . . . and maybe not. It was April who had saved it, if saving it was.

Brognola had already launched the rescue operation, prepared to abort the whole thing and yank his man the hell out of there, regardless of the consequences. Then the flash came from April, relaying the Striker's wishes in a last-minute plea. Last minute, for damned sure. The message came when they were just a block away from target central. Brognola had not decided how he would play it until he got up there and saw all those caged tigers prowling their lair, slinking back with yellow hatred blazing from their savage eyes—and then he understood the Striker as he had never understood him before —empathized as he had never done before.

To a guy confronting that sort of hellish real-

ity day in and day out, living with it and prepared to die with it . . . well, yeah, New York
was worthwhile. All of it was worthwhile.

If the guy wanted to play his only hand to the
final gasp, then who the hell was Harold Brognola to tell him nay?

And it could very well *be* the final gasp, yes.
There was still the problem of Minotti. A face-
down with that guy would very likely be disas-
trous. But evidently the Striker knew what he
was doing. Brognola hoped so. He draped his
arm chummily across Sigmund's shoulders and
walked him into the garage.

"You'n me, pal," he said quietly, "have many
things to talk about."

"It's dead, anyway," Sigmund said drearily.
"You can have whatever you want. If, of course,
I get full immunity and total security."

"You'll get what I want to give you, guy,"
Brognola told him. "Just make me happy."

"I'll make you delirious," Sigmund promised.
"Just keep me alive and well."

Minotti was in one of his crazy rages. He
kicked a glass table halfway across the lounge
and threw a vase of silk flowers at the bar, then
pulled out his revolver and emptied it into the
chair where Sigmund had sat, just a moment
ago.

The torpedoes walked around on eggs, ex-
changing dark glances and avoiding eye contact with the boss.

Leo Turrin stood against the wall near the foyer, one leg crossed in front of the other, arms at his chest and waggling his eyebrows at a nearby gunman.

Then the door over there opened; the tall man filled the opening, hardly more than a shadow against the strong sunlight spilling out from behind.

Minotti was reloading his gun. He looked up as the tall man asked, in a voice that filled the large room, "What the hell is all the racket out here?"

"I was just coming in to tell you all about it," Minotti called back. He was calm, now, the rage vented—but still looking dangerous as hell.

"So come on," said the big man. He disappeared, leaving the door open, the sunlight streaming through.

The torpedo closest to Turrin said, in quiet awe, "Jesus! Who is that?"

"That," said Turrin, just as quietly, "is the guy who's going to save your ass from crazy Marco."

So . . . the stage was set, the fix was in . . . and only God and Mack Bolan could know what might happen next.

CHAPTER 14

TURNAROUND

The guy was standing at the window, his face in half profile in the dazzling sunlight, eyes shaded by heavy sunglasses. Big guy, impressive as hell. Vaguely familiar, too . . . The damned sunglasses, maybe. Damned right! Nola had said . . .

Minotti held up at the doorway, the revolver still clasped loosely in a relaxed hand. He growled, "You're the guy hit my bathhouse awhile ago!"

The Ace replied in a quiet, clipped voice, "That's right."

Minotti squared his shoulders and yelled,

111

"Well I hope you got a damned good explanation for that crap!"

The guy shrugged and softly replied, "We still have the kid, Marco."

"*We*, hell! I don't—hold it there! What're you saying? You snatched her for *me*?"

The Death Card turned full face toward Minotti. Now he could see even less of the guy. That damned sun . . . He moved on inside the room but stayed close to the open doorway as he demanded, "Close the damned blinds!"

"In a minute," the Ace replied—explaining: "My face man says I should get ten minutes of morning sun, 'til the marks fade. First chance I've had all day, with the rain and all. They turn blue, you know, if you're not careful."

No, Minotti had not known that. So that was where the guy had been since Augie . . . getting a damned new face. Probably with very good reason, too.

Minotti growled, "What'd you mean about the kid?"

Omega turned a bit more toward the doorway as he replied, smiling, "I mean that I beat Sigmund to her by about five minutes."

Minotti could believe that! He could almost believe anything about that . . ! He said, the anger surfacing again, "Listen, Omega, I want you to put the sign on that guy! I don't care what it costs or what it takes! I want 'im hit and I want it damned quick! Even if he's in the bed with the Attorney General—wherever—

112

even if it takes an atom bomb! Get me? I want that guy *hit!*"

"It's already taken care of," Omega replied smoothly.

"Is that right! Well I . . . okay, if you say so. For now. I guess he knew you had 'im, eh? That's why the feds . . . ?"

"That's why, yeah," said the smooth bastard. "You were a godsend for him, coming in when you did. I knew he was stalling for time but I didn't know he'd already sent for help. But don't worry it, Marco. He's a dead man."

These guys, Marco knew . . . these guys like Omega and Sigmund—it did not pay to underestimate them. Mean as hell, cold like death— and a lot smarter, in certain important ways, than Marco could ever be. He knew that. But he would never accept it, not really, not down where it really counted. For now, though . . .

"Damned right he's a dead man!" Minotti yelled—speaking, also, to the gallery outside. He was working himself into another balls-out rage, encouraging it, enjoying the feeling of invincible power that it produced within him. "That son of a bitch, Omega, that double-dealing bastard, all this time telling me—I bet that's why we hit shit everywhere we turned, all this time. I bet half the time we thought it was that Bolan, it was this rotten . . ."

Minotti ran out of wind. He kicked the wall, holstered his gun then plucked it back, hit the door with it, sucked in his breath, felt his eyes begin to roll in their sockets and knew that it was time to tuck it all back in.

Omega calmly suggested, "You'll have a stroke, Marco. Leave all this worry to me, huh? You got more important things to attend to."

The guy was right. More important things. "So what about that Bolan? Hey, I meant to ask . . . what kind of car do you drive?"

"I drive a Ferrari," Omega told him.

Just like that. Minotti sucked in another breath and said, "Well, I'll be damned. Red one?"

"Last time I looked, yeah," said the guy who drives a Ferrari.

"And when was that?"

Omega shrugged and casually replied, "It's in the garage. I hope. Call down and ask your boys to see."

Minotti glared at the sun-shrouded figure at the window for a moment, then declared, "The last red Ferrari I saw was sitting up in Central Park all shot to hell!"

"Not mine," the guy said coolly, adding: "I hope. Sigmund's maybe. He's been pulling some fancy doughnuts on me, the past couple of weeks. How'd it get shot up?"

"It followed us from the bathhouse," Minotti explained, wondering what the hell. "But I also heard that the guy snatched the kid and left in a car like that. So you tell me what the hell!"

"That was the battle in the park? You? And a Ferrari?"

"That's right," said Minotti, squinting at that shadowy figure.

"You better check the garage," Omega said quietly.

Damned right he'd better. Minotti stepped back into the open doorway and called out, "Matty! Call down and see if Omega's Ferrari is there." Then, to Omega: "I don't see how . . . How far did you take the kid?"

"Not far," the Ace replied. "I was back here within about ten minutes after I left your joint. I didn't see Sigmund around, though. Maybe he was tailing me, the whole time. Maybe he slipped in, ripped off my car, and slipped out again. But let's see what Matty has to say."

Omega had not moved from his position at the window, but he'd turned the other side of his face to the sun. Minotti wished he could get a better look at the guy, without making an issue of it. These guys were always a bit touchy about . . . Dammit, though, he sure looked familiar!

"I put the kid on ice, Marco," he was saying. "She's pretty sick. I think we almost lost her. Don't worry it, though. She's in good hands, now."

Which reminded Minotti of something else. He cried, aghast, "Not that goddam Eisener, I hope! I think maybe Sigmund had that guy in the pocket, too!"

Omega replied, "Not Eisener, no. A real doctor. Don't worry, she's cool. Until you need her. Just tell me when."

Marco would tell the guy when, damned right. How 'bout, by God, right now? He was about to say just that when the guy diverted him with another troubling point.

"How do you figure Sigmund found out about her?"

"Same way I did, maybe," Minotti replied, thinking about it, though. "How did you find out?"

"I was spotting Sigmund," Omega quietly explained.

"Well you do damned good work, guy, I'll say that. Listen . . . you and I got to get the heads together and get this mess unscrewed. Hope I can count on you for that."

"It could depend on the girl, Marco," said the cool bastard.

"Us getting together depends on . . ?"

"No, I mean unscrewed. She could be crucial."

No, Minotti guessed not. He told the guy as much, adding: "I think it was all part of that rotten bastard's razzle dazzle, anyway. Come to think of it, Omega, why don't you just sit on that kid for me 'til I find out what it's all about. And, uh, I 'preciate the thought—I mean, what you did for me. We can—"

"Where'd you find her, Marco?"

"Huh?"

"The kid."

"You don't know?"

"How would I know? She was in a coma when I picked her up. Still is, maybe."

"A coma?"

"That's right. Your friend Eisener . . ."

The anger was flaring again. Minotti gnashed his teeth and said, "The fink! Probably trying to kill her, behind my back! Well, to hell with it! That's all dumb history, now."

"I think it may be important," Omega persisted. "With Sigmund now in the open . . . And he knows about the kid. How embarrassing could that get?"

Minotti wavered, deciding maybe he should tell the guy all about it, when Matty Carzone moved quietly to the doorway and whispered in his ear: "A red Ferrari is in the garage, okay. Clean as a whistle. But you should know, also, that Johnny Grazzi and his Brooklyn commandos are all over the place. I guess Johnny is on his way up, right now."

"Tell the boys to cool it," Minotti whispered back. "Greet them like brothers. I'll be with you in a minute."

He turned back to the big cool figure at the window. The guy was lowering the blinds now, his ten minutes in the sun obviously satisfied. Now Minotti could see even less, in the sudden gloom, his eyes flaring into the adjustment.

"We'll talk about the kid later, Omega," Minotti told the shadow. "Our friends from Brooklyn just came in. Give me five minutes, then I want you to come out and say hello. Let's nail this thing down, right here and now."

The guy replied, very softly, "You're right. The time has come."

Damned right the time had come. Minotti growled, "Five minutes, eh?"

"Right," said the shadow. "Meanwhile, send Leo in here, will you?"

Minotti spun through the doorway and rejoined his boys, in the lounge. He was still a bit troubled about this Omega guy . . . something . . . something out of whack . . . something . . .

Leo said, "He's an okay guy, isn't he, Marco?"

"Yeah, yeah," replied Marco, but still wondering if it was true. "Uh, he wants to see you, Leo. You say the guy worked for you before?"

"For all of us, Marco. He brought his own organization down around his ears to protect us from it."

"You mean . . ?"

"I mean the Aces, sure. Barney had the whole outfit wired like puppets. Omega is the guy that snipped those wires. Ask Billy Gino. He was closer to it than I was."

"Where is Billy?"

"I think he's downstairs visiting with some of your boys. You know Billy. A brother is everything."

"Yeah, sure, good man," Minotti growled.

"Uh, look, I got to talk to Grazzi. Tell Billy I'd like to talk to him, too—pretty quick, eh?"

Minotti went on, then, and called his boys around him. Something did not smell good. Off key, off key. It jangled at the nerves and made Marco want to hit somebody.

Something, yeah, was very wrong here.

CHAPTER 15

ONCE UPON A TIME . . .

Bolan had never ceased to be amazed by the frailty of human perceptions. Just three days earlier he had stood toe to toe with Marco Minotti in a trailer near White Sands—in a quite different pose, of course, but toe to toe, nonetheless—and parleyed with the guy for several minutes.

Shortly thereafter, Minotti had to have known that the mysterious "Architect" of White Sands was none other than Mack Bolan. In all fairness, though, Bolan had to allow for the fact that the role at White Sands was considerably removed from the role here. Also, one "sees" with more than the eye which is, after all, hardly more than a camera lens. It is the brain that takes those shifting patterns of light and converts them into a comprehensible structure—and, beyond the brain, it is the mind itself which lends meaning to that structure.

So Minotti "saw," in that office, essentially what he had been prepared to see—helped in every way possible, of course, by Bolan's own creative manipulation of the "patterns of light" available in there.

He had figured it at a fifty-fifty chance for success. And he knew very well that Minotti had walked away from it with a fuzzy and troubled focus. Such sleight-of-hand could not work forever, of course. And Bolan did not wish to give the guy too much further opportunity to resolve the focus of that troubled mind.

So when Leo stepped into the office, Bolan told him, "It's getting tight, buddy. I'm losing it. How many guns are out there?"

Turrin worriedly reported, "In the lounge, right now, maybe twenty. I make it another twenty or so scattered between here and the garage. And it's getting worse. Grazzi has arrived. I would guess he has close to thirty or more of his own. We can't count on them cancelling each other out—even though, of course, these are shaky times for family loyalty. All of those guys are nervous as hell. I do get the feeling that there is not a lot of confidence in Marco—and if he is having that kind of trouble, you can imagine how Grazzi is set, with even weaker credentials. So hell, I just don't know. I do know this much: Marco is in a bargaining mood. He's brokering openly and with all the persuasive charm a guy like that can muster. But he's psycho as hell, Sarge. They all know it, too. I'd say that's your only chance. I don't see how you could shoot your way out unless they start shooting at each other first."

"Well, that's a thought," Bolan mused.

"Okay, but I got something else, too. Don't know if it could be any help right now but . . ."

"What?" Bolan asked quietly.

"Does the name Lou Nola mean something to you?"

"A lot, yeah."

"Okay," Turrin said. "He called. Here's the message. A guy named Artie Johnson, a free-lancer, snatched the kid. Marco sent this Johnson down to Washington last Tuesday night, just before Marco himself left for New Mexico. A guy named Eisener and a couple of local punks went with Johnson. They got back from Washington on Wednesday night. Johnson and his two punks were fished out of the East River on Thursday, inside the car they took to Washington. Nola says this is solid and it's worth a lot more than a grand."

"A lot, yeah," Bolan said thoughtfully. "Did Nola say where he got this?"

"He got it from Eisener. Eisener, whoever, is

scared out of his skull and running. Wants your protection. I told Nola to call back in an hour. What do you think?"

"I think," Bolan replied softly, "that I would love to discuss this with Mr. Eisener right now. Did Nola leave a number?"

"Hell no. He's like a rabbit on Fifth Avenue, himself. Says that Marco has crews out scouring the town for this Eisener guy."

"If he calls again, Leo, send them to Hal."

"Okay. But does it make a difference here?"

"It could," Bolan replied, still skulling it.

"Just who is this kid?"

"Wish to hell I knew," said Bolan. "I can't help feeling . . . some sort of trump hand Minotti was trying to . . . has to be, something . . . he and Sigmund were tight and getting tighter until . . . Washington, uh huh."

"What does *Uh-huh* mean?"

"I don't know, Leo. At the same time, I do know. Like Minotti and his fuzzy . . . it's there but I can't see it, yet, not clearly. Sigmund has been commuting to Washington the past two weeks. He found a leak in our system and was beginning to puzzle it out. He confided in Marco —but, he says, not totally. Marco . . ."

"Marco what?" Turrin prodded.

"Marco has been making a damned lot of noise, lately, hasn't he."

"Coming on," Turrin replied, "like Augie Junior."

"He's cagey, that guy," Bolan mused. "Dangerous as a snake, too. Doesn't trust Omega. Wouldn't have trusted Sigmund, either, whatever the bond. Trump hand. Yeah. Okay. He muscled it. That has to be the answer, Leo, part of it. He muscled Sigmund's delicate Washington operation. Moved in on it. But why didn't Sigmund know? Who the hell *is* that kid?"

"There's no time to go public with it," Turrin commented, ". . . or else maybe we could find out."

Bolan had come to some sort of decision. He checked his appearance and said, "Walk me to the terrace, Leo."

Turrin nervously replied, "You're sure you want to go out there?"

"I'm sure, yeah. Straight through them, all the way to the terrace. Talk it up, laugh it up, but don't let anyone stop us."

"What are you—?"

"I have," Bolan told him, anticipating the question, "a weak radio sewed into my coat. I want a parley with Hal. I need the terrace for radio stretch. Too much steel around us, in here. I need the open air of the terrace. So let's go."

They went, arm in arm across the lounge, chatting quietly about old times, better times— the impressive Ace of Spades with his consort, Sir Leo of the Lion Heart—graciously accepting quiet greetings of respect and admiration as they traversed that savage turf.

Minotti and Grazzi were in a tight-two parley at a table in the far corner, speaking soberly and animatedly of, no doubt, worldshaking matters of Mafia state while their respective close-cadres glared suspiciously at one another just out of earshot of the parley at the table.

Turrin closed the terrace door behind them with a quiet sigh of relief and muttered, "I told you. They're getting it together."

Bolan pulled him to the parapet and they stood there at arms-length distance, apparently engaged in quiet conversation as Bolan touched his lapel and spoke to the shoulder.

"Striker Base."

Immediately, crisply, at the ear: "Babysitter here."

She must have been sitting there waiting for it, microphone in hand.

Bolan's request was terse and to the point: "Quick parley with the Wonderland Kid."

"Moment," she shot back. "Alice is . . . one moment. We've been concerned! Is it okay with you?"

"Warm and getting warmer," he responded. "I need that parley, the quickest."

"I am making the connection. Stand by one."

Bolan stood by, grinning at Turrin and apparently reacting to the showtalk which had continued unabated from that good friend.

Then, at the ear, Brognola: "Alice here. A-OK at my end. The guy is singing his entire repertoire."

Into the shoulder: "I need the Wonderland connection. Who is the girl?"

"Is she connected to that?" inquired the ear.

"I'm asking you. I think so, yeah. Ask the man."

"Already did. Knows nothing about it, or so he says. Is it important?"

"Could be, yes. She was snatched from Wonderland Tuesday night or Wednesday. Where is your subject now?"

"In my van, giving a concert. Good thing we came to town, pal. For what it's worth, I'm dining on crow right now. You were right. The Apple is worth it. Our house was built upon shifting sands. More on that, later. How can I support?"

Bolan threw a glance at the glass wall. Two guys were standing just inside, hands in pockets, watching while not watching.

He told the shoulder, "The shifting sands are the key. Get the guy to sharpen his repertoire. Also, take some Polaroids of your medical case and fax them to Wonderland. Circulate the Polaroids to the inner circle—or call that the *oval* circle. I'm betting someone will recognize her. I think she was Marco's trump. Try it that way and get it back to me with all haste."

"All haste, right," Brognola agreed. "Meanwhile . . ."

Bolan glanced again into the lounge. "Meanwhile," he told the shoulder, "another show of force could save the day without breaking it. Just a show, though, not a full war dance. On the street, below, maybe."

127

"Gotcha," replied the friend from Wonderland. "Give it two minutes then look out the window."

"I'll be looking."

He gave it a brief pause then said, "Cool it there, Babysitter. It's well in hand."

"Just wait 'til it gets into *my* hands," came the purring promise. "Keep it healthy, please."

Bolan chuckled, touched the lapel and moved the hand on to playfully slap at Turrin's cheek.

Leo, of course, had heard only half of that conversation—and probably not much of that part. "So?" he asked, as they strolled back toward the lounge. "Did you get any comfort?"

"There will be a show of force on the streets below in about two minutes," Bolan reported soberly through smiling lips. "That means we should start something of our own to mesh with that. Got any ideas?"

"Something wild."

"Something wild is right," Bolan replied, smiling on. "Something, maybe, as crazy as Marco."

"Guess I know what you mean," Leo said, staring straight ahead. "I've been thinking about it for most of an hour, now."

They stepped inside.

Leo slid the door shut with a bang.

"Omega" winked at a Minotti hardman, took Leo by the arm and said, loud enough for those nearby to overhear, "I'll tell you an interesting story, Leo. Once upon a time, see, there was this Wise Man from the East. He thought he had the world by the ass, see, but all that he had was a tiger by the tail."

"Once upon a time, eh?" Turrin said, just as loudly—throwing knowing looks to all within range.

"Well, of course," Omega replied, with heavy emphasis, "that *time* is *now*."

CHAPTER 16

SHOW OF FORCE

The Minotti-Grazzi parley was evidently going pretty well. The two principals were relaxed in their chairs, sipping wine, all smiles. The pleasant atmosphere was siphoning off, also, onto the cadres. The "boys" were prowling less, standing off in relaxed groups—though still separated by family lines—obviously very much relieved that the tensions were abating.

Minotti's "close-cadre"—the human shields—had taken a table and were sitting in a more or less relaxed attitude some twenty feet away from their boss.

At the bar, about twenty feet in the opposite direction, stood Grazzi's pledged flesh.

Bolan murmured to Leo Turrin, "So start it," and dropped away to jaw pleasantly with a Minotti group who stood near the foyer door.

Turrin lit a cigarette, went to the east window and paused there for a moment, looking down, then hurried to the bar and tapped Grazzi's bodycock, one Charlie Atlantic, on the shoulder. "How's it going?" he asked quietly.

"Looks okay," the bodycock replied soberly. "What do you think?"

"I think," Leo told that guy, "that we should not forget the old proverbs. How does that one go?—when the wine begins to flow, the blood cannot be far behind? You remember that one?"

The guy stiffened somewhat and said, "Yeah. Don't worry, I'm watching it."

"Come watch something else, then," Leo suggested, "if you got a quick second."

Charlie Atlantic told his boys, "Don't budge," and went with Turrin to the east window. From there, at a point where the terrace began, was an excellent view of the area surrounding Rockefeller Plaza, just up the street. But that street was curiously free of traffic, except for two large buses which were pulled up at the plaza. Tiny figures in khaki clothing were moving around, down there, and it looked as though the street was being barricaded.

Charlie Atlantic grunted and produced collapsible opera glasses from his coat pocket, opened them, and raised the glasses to his eyes.

"Is it what I'm afraid it is?" Turrin inquired softly.

"If you're afraid of feds, then you're right," the bodycock assured him. He passed the glasses over. "I thought those guys had left. We just missed 'em, coming in. What the hell does it mean?"

Turrin was peering through the glasses, working hard to suppress a smile of admiration for his boss, the Whiz from Wonderland. It could not have been a better "show of force." Marshals in flak jackets and carrying riot guns were moving into position all along the plaza area, forming into squads, apparently preparing to move out. "I guess," Leo told his "pal" from Brooklyn, "it means they're coming back. I wonder if they are barricading all around us?"

"I just wonder what it means," Charlie Atlantic commented nervously.

"Well, I have to wonder if *Marco* could tell us what it means," Leo said, handing back the opera glasses and arching his eyebrows for added meaning.

"What the hell would *he* stand to gain by .. ?"

Turrin shrugged his shoulders. "All I know, Charlie, is that they came up before and took one guy away. One guy who Marco could not get into the pocket. And I guess they're coming back. There's nobody here, now, Charlie, who was not here before. 'Cept, of course, Johnny Grazzi and the best of Brooklyn."

"That doesn't sound . . ."

"It never does," Turrin replied archly. "Who knows where the clout goes, these days, eh?"

The big bodycock growled something unintelligible and hurried back toward the bar.

Some of Minotti's boys had naturally noted the action at the window with the opera glasses. Four of them drifted casually onto the terrace and went straight to the parapet. Two of those came quickly back inside and began to circulate among the cadre.

These quiet tensions were quickly communicated to the men at the bosses' table. Both were beginning to quiver with tightening nerves when a guy hurried over and whispered something in Minotti's ear.

He immediately pulled his revolver and rose halfway out of his chair.

In the immediate wake of that reaction, before anyone could actually read the intention there, at that table, the four men at the bar opened fire on the four Minotti bodyguards, who had reacted quickly to the sight of their boss's firearm and were scrambling to their feet.

Those four had not all hit the floor yet when Minotti himself began emptying his leaping revolver into the stupefied person of Johnny Grazzi.

Then, of course, it all went crazy.

Leo made a dive for cover behind an overstuffed lounge, near the wall.

Bolan had already begun his move and he

was several paces removed from Omega's office when the shooting started. That whole penthouse was a hellground when he reappeared in the office doorway with the M-79 raised and ready. He sent a round of HE toward the glass wall at the terrace, then quickly reloaded and sent another.

That whole side of the room was immediately obscured behind clouds of flame and smoke. Elsewhere, guys were diving around and staggering around, firing weapons in every direction, flinging blood in gushing torrents everywhere.

It was enough. It was, hell, too much.

Bolan introduced some chemical smoke into the situation, then a round of teargas as he moved swiftly toward the foyer door.

Someone ran past him when he was about halfway across, someone grunting and wheezing with fear and the stretch for survival—and a combat shiver suggested to him that this "someone" was Crazy Marco. But he was diverted from that prey by a familiar voice at his right flank. It was Leo, pleading for a cease-fire.

Bolan worked his way through the acrid smoke toward the sound of that voice, grabbed his friend by the arm, and pulled him toward the exit.

The occasional boom of a heavy handgun could still be heard reverberating through the insanity when they reached the foyer and groped their way toward the stairway door. The elevator car, of course, was gone—and Bolan knew that it would not be coming back up, not for a while.

There were other feet on that stairwell, too, maybe a floor below. A pistol down there boomed and sent a slug gouging into the plaster above Bolan's head, then a door down there banged shut. Whoever—Marco, maybe—was scrambling for the other elevators.

Bolan and Turrin went on down, cautiously, past the 27th and to the 26th. An elevator was on the way down, the floor indicators showing the progress. Bolan called another car, grimly avoiding his friend's dazed eyes, then stepped aboard and punched off.

"The garage?" Leo asked, unbelieving.

"Why not?" Bolan replied gruffly. "That's where the future is at. I think it's Marco, ahead of us. I think he knows too much. About tomorrow, maybe. I can't give him that."

"God, no," agreed the Sticker. "We've worked too hard for it."

But Mack Bolan was dining on a bit of crow, himself. Brognola had been right, too. The Phoenix Project was too vitally important to be allowed to fall apart in America's own junglelands. He had to catch that guy. And he had to pin the mark of the beast across that insane mouth. Otherwise, the Wonderland politicians would have a field day with a besieged president, another morbid government crisis would probably ensue, and there would be no Phoenix

Project now or ever, with Mack Bolan or any-one else at the helm.

The savages of the world would just go on eating the gentle folk, and the civilized world would . . .

Okay, yeah, say it—melodrama or not.

The civilized world would begin to eat itself.

CHAPTER 17

ON BOLAN

The underground garage was a small hellground, too, when they reached it.

Handguns were sounding off with much larger voices than their powder commanded, amplified and echoing in the cavernous environment, sending their hot little messengers pounding into or ricocheting from the hapless metallic beasts entrapped there.

A couple of those cars were screeching about on straining rubber, fighting for traction and an avenue conducive to a safe retreat. As one of those reached the ramp, the other lost control and banged into a steel stanchion, then hurtled away only to slam broadside into a parked vehicle. Both cars involved in that pileup erupted into a flashing explosion which hurled chunks of shredded metal far and wide, impacting the flesh, also, with the shock wave from that contained blast.

Bolan and Turrin took advantage of that diversion to break down the line to the red Ferrari, parked about ten spaces beyond the office by one of Brognola's people. Bolan fished the keys from behind the license plate and they were aboard and making some screeches of their own by the time the gunfight resumed.

There was no way to know, in all the confusion, who was fighting whom—but the general identity of the participants seemed rather obvious: it was still Minotti versus Grazzi, in a family sense.

They were jockeying past the burning vehicles when a nearby pistol spat two slugs screaming past their windshield. Then someone in the background yelled, "That's Omega in the Ferrari! Let 'im pass!"

"Who was that?" Bolan grunted as they raced up the ramp toward daylight.

"Beats me," Leo grunted back. "Billy Gino, maybe."

"Say a prayer for Billy, then," Bolan suggested.

They hit the street and screamed about in a tire-testing skid toward the opposite curb. The impact there straightened the plunge and sent them hurtling off in hot pursuit of a heavy sedan which had just quit the hellgrounds and was now plowing through the sawhorse barricades at the intersection north.

"I'm dropping you at the barricades!" Bolan announced.

"Like hell you are!" Turrin yelled back.

There was no sense in both of them taking the chase. Besides, Leo had never been a combat type. Mob politics was his specialty, not death on the run.

Bolan explained, "I want you to brief Hal! Tell him to track my progress and close with all possible speed! If we lose this guy, now . . ."

"How do you know it's him?" Leo protested. "It could be anybody in that car!"

"I have to play the worst! He should also contain the action back there and make sure none slip through!"

They had penetrated the intersection, swerving around the remains of the sawhorse barricade, and Bolan was already applying the brakes when a heightened drama ahead began to unfold. Two of Brognola's big buses suddenly pulled broadside across the street just opposite Rockefeller Plaza, creating an entirely effective barricade to contain the fleeing sedan at that point.

The Mafia vehicle tried to leap the curb and go around but instead found deep trouble on the plaza itself. It grazed a light standard, then ran up onto a low wall, suspended there with all four wheels still turning but something that looked like the driveshaft lying on the ground alongside.

Three guys leapt away from there, ignoring a distant challenge from Brognola's marshals, and ran into the plaza.

One of those guys, yeah, was definitely Crazy Marco. The Ferrari skidded to a halt, Bolan yelled to Turrin, "Tell Hal!" and erupted from there as though shot from his own gun.

Turrin sat there for a moment and inspected his shaking hands, then he picked up the cut-down M-79 which Bolan had left on the seat and stood up to test his legs.

They were doing exactly what the hands were doing; Leo had to admit, if only to himself, that he was not cut out for this kind of work.

Brognola was running up from the shredded barricades, all wild-eyed and breathing like a novice marathon runner at race's end. He stopped running when he saw Turrin, coming on at a more sedate pace and calling ahead, breathlessly, "Thank God you're okay. Where the hell is Striker?"

A suggested answer to that question came from the plaza, in the form of volleying pistol fire. "He's chasing Marco," Turrin reported. "He says the guy knows about tomorrow, maybe. He wants all possible support. But you'd better call the uniforms off, Hal. They—"

But Brognola was already moving on, running full-out again toward a squad of heavily armed marshals who were beginning to cautiously advance upon the plaza.

"They might gun him down," Turrin continued, voicing his worry aloud, anyway, to an empty street.

But then a familiar vehicle turned through that deserted intersection back there, and a familiar, pretty lady stepped down from it a moment later.

"He turned his beeper on!" she called to Leo. "Get that damned bus out of my way!"

But the bus was already moving clear, propelled by a marshal in uniform.

Leo ran to the Warwagon and leapt inside just before the door closed on him.

They were moving in a quick acceleration as he struggled to his feet, putting Rockefeller Plaza swiftly to the rear.

"Where away?" Leo panted.

"Tracking north," the pretty lady called back to him. "On foot, I'm sure. Are you armed?"

"Sort of," Leo replied feebly.

"Armory is in the rear, soldier! Use it!"

The "soldier," by God, went back there and used it. He took a Uzi, strapped on a readybelt and took on extra clips of ammo. He could hear the lady, up forward, trying to raise Hal on the radio.

It was time for all good men to rally 'round. And Leo, by God—cut from the right cloth or not—was ready to do or die.

If Bolan should lose it now—if, God forbid, he should die on this last lousy day in hell, then . . .

Leo shoved in the clip, armed the little weapon and went forward to stand ready at the door.

"Do you have his signal?" he asked the lady.

"Now and then," she replied. "It seems that they are moving through null areas, here and there. Through buildings, maybe, I don't know."

That pretty voice was strained with an agony similar, Leo was sure, to his own.

Similar, sure; but not the same.

She loved the guy.

Of course, Leo loved him, too. Not in the same way, course not, but love just the same.

Then he heard that good voice, clear as a bell as it lifted away from a speaker above the con, a bit breathless but clear nonetheless.

"Moving north toward Central Park, Eighth Avenue," it reported. "Are you on me?"

Leo could see her lips trembling against the mike and wondered how the words came so clear as she responded to that. "We're on you, Striker. Be careful, dammit."

But Leo the Sticker knew that the Striker would not, could not, be "careful." A daylight chase along the busy Manhattan streets could not ever be that, not for a guy in Bolan's shoes. Somewhere along the way, a cop and then a whole parade of cops would join that chase, and then . . .

"Get closer!" Leo urged the lady. "And keep on trying to raise Hal. Drop me as soon as we hit the fire zone. Maybe I can at least backdoor the guy and protect the rear, if nothing else."

The "Sticker" was a sticker no longer.

The thing he'd been sticking to all these years was now a dead thing, of that he was certain. And all the hell had been worth it.

But not with Bolan dead.

It would all come up ashes, that way.

So Leo Turrin was now, by God, a "Striker." And he would strike anything or anybody who tried to foreclose Mack Bolan's final victory in hell.

Yes. He would strike even himself.

CHAPTER 18

MEDITATION

There was no "fire zone" out here, on these civilized streets. Leo Turrin and April Rose would know that for themselves, in a moment. As for Mack Bolan, his weapon was sheathed and he was merely concentrating on keeping the guy in sight. He had a pretty good idea where Minotti was headed. Toward Roman Nights, no doubt. Even charred in spots and watersoaked, the "favorite toy" would beckon magnetically to a guy whose bubble had burst so dramatically, so devastatingly, so quickly. Maybe the guy even had some money stashed there—or some other comfort. Whatever, Bolan was pretty sure that the trail would end there.

Minotti had been working his way toward that imagined haven, on a zigzag course which finally stabilized along 8th Avenue, for more than ten minutes since the gunfight at Rockefeller Plaza. The last of his "boys" had lent their blood to the artistic fountains there and left their boss woefully alone in a world he could no longer manipulate.

The guy was crazy, sure.

And he was obviously moving, now, through some mental world of his own creation. Not once had he tried for a cab, or looked at a bus. Crazy Marco was walking home—or, if the stories were true, to the closest thing to a home he had known throughout all his savage life.

The gossip was that, tucked away behind the stairwell on the first floor of the building housing Roman Nights, there was a "play house" where Marco sometimes took a special lady—special, that is, for the night. And, according to the stories, that Roman Nights apartment was done up like a turn of the century mansion—like, perhaps, something that a very young boy had seen once in a movie or in a magazine. It was sad, sure, and even tragic—but the sadness did not remove the monster from the man who had once been a deprived boy.

It simply underscored the social brutalizations which created monsters like Marco Minotti. All the tears and moral arguments the world could produce would not change the present fact that Marco was an incorrigible and deadly enemy of the American dream. He would take what he could seize, kill what pleased him to destroy, brutalize as he himself had been brutalized until someone finally, mercifully, removed Marco from the human family. He had no place there, now, and none could be made for him.

Bolan did not "hate" such men. The sadness which he often felt for them could not be matched by professional moralists or social designers. He hated, of course, what these men represented. And sometimes he hated the social ills that bred them, a civilized world that would not police itself, a "gentle" society which preferred to hide its face and hope that the monsters would all go away.

They would not go away.

Anyone who had lingered awhile in the savage jungles of America's underbelly knew that they would not go away. They would prey and prey and go on preying until the last gentle man took his hands from his eyes to see the final blow which split his skull and killed forever the promised inheritance of the meek.

How could the "meek" ever hope to inherit a savage earth? Surely not—unless, of course, a fingersnap from heaven could set it all straight.

But would that fingersnap reform the savage and fill the animal breast with love instead of lust? Hardly. If that hand from heaven ever did come down, it would surely smash all the savages everywhere, once and for all.

Bolan could not believe in fingersnaps from heaven. It was his personal conviction that God had built the world for men to tame—and women, too, of course—and to build themselves into something *worthy* of survival during the taming process.

Some day, sure, maybe, if all went well and the process continued, the world would be a safe place for soft men and women. At present, it was not. Whatever safety there was had been bought and paid for by *hard* men and women.

And yes, there were those times, too, when Mack Bolan felt a surge of resentment toward the soft ones, those who shrank with horror of the real world into their silk cocoons of golden dreams and premature platitudes in a world too soft to police itself. Those were the ones who made necessary the personal commitments and lonely hells shared by those who were willing to face the savage realities of a world not yet ready for paradise.

Someone, here and there, had to stand hard . . . forever. And, yes, a single individual could sometimes turn the tide of savagery . . . if there was, at least, moral support from the land of golden dreams.

Look east, soft ones, and look west. Look north and south, up and down, and tell Mack Bolan where paradise lies. Find a place where competition is gone, where weapons of war are obsolete, where gloating savages do not lurk in darkened doorways, where undisciplined greed does not suppress compassion and generosity.

But if you know of no such place . . . do not then begrudge the hard man who knows the truth and puts his blood where his conscience lies.

Bolan snapped himself from the meditations of a mind weary of blood and death—the inevitable meditations, perhaps, of a principled man who thought as well as he fought.

There were no "warm sties" here, for Mack Bolan.

He had to kill again—and he had to do it in a particularly brutal way. Not with any sense of pleasure, no. A civilized warrior would take no falsely moral view of the necessary suppression of the crazies of this tired world.

He simply did what he had to do.

And Bolan had to kill a crazy—in a way which would give some positive meaning to the kill.

CHAPTER 19

THE HARD MEN

It was, yes, a Victorian parlor—faithfully reproduced with genuine antiques and all the trimmings of that gracious age—beautiful even though now waterlogged and soggy underfoot.

A strange place, indeed, for Crazy Marco. But why all hidden away like this? Why not . . ?

Bolan decided to ask the horse's mouth.

"Beautiful place, Marco," he said softly. "So why do you hide it from the world?"

The ex-boss whirled around like a frightened child caught with his hand inside the cookie jar.

But this "frightened child" was, at that very

moment, trying to mate a drum-magazine to the belly of an old Thompson submachine gun.

"Omega!" he gasped. "Christ's sake, you scared the hell out of me!"

Bolan's weapon was in its shoulder holster. He stepped forward, took the Thompson from that dazed grasp, opened the breech and inserted the magazine, handed it back. "Be careful with that thing," he warned. "It's primed to go. You ever fired it?"

"Course I've fired it!" Marco replied huffily, but his eyes avoiding contact with Bolan's. "It's a fine piece, isn't it, really fine. My brother Frank gave it to me for my birthday when I turned seventeen. Manhood, he said, I was ready for it. He took it off a dead G-man. And, listen, that was in the days when a G-man was a *Gee*-man. They were tough, in those days."

"They're still tough, Marco," Bolan told him. "When they're allowed to be."

"Bull."

"Well," said Bolan/Omega, rubbing his hands together, "it's been a hell of a day, hasn't it."

"The devil took it," said Crazy Marco.

"So it's been a hell of a day, that's what I said."

"Not yet it hasn't," Marco said slyly.

"No?"

"No."

"What do you have in mind for the Thompson?"

"I'm going hunting."

"Yeah? Where?"

"Right outside."

"In the park? No way, Marco. You can't go hunting in Central Park."

"I didn't say the park. I said outside. It's something I've always wanted to do—you know? I want to just open this baby up and blast something, just once, just open 'er up and let 'er rip, don't let off on the trigger 'til the drum is empty. Frank did that once, he said. Did you know Frank?"

"Yes, I knew him," said Frank's executioner.

"Hell of a guy, wasn't he! Best big brother a kid could ask for! Took me out and got me laid in the fanciest whorehouse in town when I was only thirteen years old. We'd sit up all night playing blackjack or acey-ducey, getting drunker'n a skunk—night after night when he was layin' low, sometimes—and sometimes we'd bring some broads in and party all night. Hell, I was thirteen. Well, listen—I was tellin' you— he opened this baby up, that time, tore the hell out of about a dozen cars and two beer trucks, killed I guess fifty or sixty men and—"

"That's pure bullshit, Marco," Bolan said, hoping to shock the guy back to reality.

"Like hell it is!"

"Sure it is. Think about it. How many rounds does that drum carry?"

"Well, maybe he used a couple."

Bolan shook his head. "Not even then, no way."

The guy was, perhaps, too far beyond the edge, this time. "You calling Frank a liar?"

"If he told you that, sure," Bolan replied easily. "You were just a kid, Marco. He was trying to impress you."

"Frank never lied to me," Minotti insisted. He carefully placed the Thompson on a graceful Victorian sofa, went to a chair, dropped into it, picked up an ancient copy of *National Geographic* from a side table, flashed the magazine at Bolan, said, "They got naked broads in these magazines. Know that? The first *Playboy*."

But he was beginning to sound almost sane, less juvenile.

Bolan told him, "I killed Frank, Marco."

"What?"

"I'm the one that killed Frank."

"Why?"

Bolan shrugged. "Seemed the thing to do."

"Uh huh. You're not really Omega, are you. You're Bolan, huh. I remember you, now. You had white sideburns, though, and nutty eyebrows." The madman chuckled. "Have to hand it to you, too. You sure scared the hell out of old ironpants. Killed 'im, too, didn't you."

Bolan replied, "Yes, I did."

"You kill 'em all."

"All I can, sure."

"That was you at Baltimore, yesterday."

Bolan nodded confirmation of that suspicion. "And Florida. All the others, this past week."

"Why?"

"Why what?" Bolan asked.

"Why this big hard-on for our Thing. We did nothing to you, asked nothing of you. So why the hard-on?"

Bolan shrugged his shoulders. "You boys just affect me that way, Marco."

"You're hot for our bodies, eh?"

"You could say that. I can't sleep at night thinking about you boys out ravaging the land. You do bad things, Marco."

"If we didn't, someone else would. We do it better, though. Anyway, who're you to talk? How many men *you* killed today, wiseguy?"

"Not nearly enough," replied the Executioner.

"You want me, now, eh?"

"That's right."

"So take me. I'm easy. What're you waiting for?"

"I want you to tell me something."

"Like what?"

"Like where'd you find the kid? Who does she belong to?"

Minotti chuckled again. "That's old history. But it *was* neat, wasn't it."

"I won't know if you don't tell me."

"I'll tell you. Why shouldn't I tell you?"

"So tell."

Crazy Marco was actually enjoying this. He flashed a big smile, fished out a cigar, searched for his lighter, asked, "Got a light?"

Bolan tossed him a book of matches.

He lit the cigar, sent a smoke ring toward the

ornate Victorian ceiling, said, "Ever hear the name Martin Thomas?"

Bolan had, but the name would not fix in his mind immediately. He said, "Tell me about 'im."

"Hey, you don't keep up with politics, do you. He's one of the top aides to the President of these United States."

Uh-huh, okay. Bolan looked appropriately impressed, without even working at it, and replied, "You're right, that's very neat. You really had Sigmund snockered, didn't you."

"Damned right. He wasn't going to pull that shit on Marco Minotti. You guys—*them* guys, them Aces think their crap comes out in rainbow colors. I got news, it comes out just like everybody else's. And smells just as bad."

"You could have dumped Sigmund any time, once you got the kid."

"That's right, I could."

"So what were you waiting for?"

Minotti gestured with his cigar as he replied, "No need for hurry. I wasn't worried. Let *them* worry for a while. Right?"

Bolan said, pointedly, "Meanwhile, the kid . . ."

"She was feeling no pain. Born with a damned silver spoon up her ass, anyway. I got no stomach for these society broads."

"She's just a kid, Marco," Bolan reminded him.

"But growing fast. Did you see those tits? Coming along okay, wouldn't you say? Hell, I was only thirteen when I got my first real piece. That kid is a good fifteen or sixteen."

"One of the gentle folk," Bolan said quietly, despairingly.

"Bullshit!" Minotti snorted. "There ain't no so-called gentle ladies or gentle men, if that's what you mean! They're all made out of the same stuff as you'n me. This Thomas guy? Know what *he* wanted? *He* wanted little boys! Yeah! Now isn't that a disgusting goddam!—listen— if Sigmund hadn't pegged onto the guy he would've disgraced the whole country! Imagine, a presidential aide!"

Bolan growled, "That's what Sigmund had on 'im, eh?"

"Sure it was. The guy's been hauled up a couple of times on molestation charges. Always managed to buy it off, quieten it down. Even his wife left him, a few years ago. She knew. Hell, she knew."

"How did Sigmund know?"

"You guys got your own ways. How the hell would I know. But you got to admit, it was mighty sweet. It was a natural."

"I guess it was," Bolan replied, sadly.

"So you see what kind of people we got in Washington!"

"Not nearly all," Bolan said quietly.

"Yeah, all," Marco insisted. "They're all out for number one. Not just Washington. Everywhere. Don't tell me different 'cause I'll never believe it. I know better. How the hell d'you

159

think I make all my money? They call me Crazy Marco, sometimes, when they think I can't hear. I always hear. Hey. Who's crazy? Guys like me?—or guys like you?"

"Sometimes I wonder, Marco," Bolan admitted. "But this is not one of those times." He slipped the Beretta from the shoulder holster. "Would you like to do your Thompson? In here? Just once, for old times sake?"

Minotti puffed thoughtfully on the cigar, studying that impassive face and trying to read some fine nuance there, his eyes now entirely sane and under control.

"You'd let me do that?" he asked, finally.

"You lived a hard life," Bolan told him. "I'll say this, you were never soft, not even when you should have been. It's okay with me if you want to go out the same way."

"I can shoot the joint up?"

"If you wish."

"Okay, I wish. How do you know I won't shoot you up with it?"

"Because I'll be standing right behind you, Marco, this Beretta at your neck. Behave yourself and I'll give you the whole drum before I pull my trigger. Otherwise . . . you'll get a damned short drum."

Minotti carefully placed his cigar in an ashtray, got to his feet, and said, "I want to empty it."

Bolan went to the sofa and snared the Thompson, clicked the safety off as he returned to the frozen mobster, went behind him and put the old chopper in the man's hands.

"You had the safety on," Minotti observed, chuckling.

"Sure," Bolan replied. "I'm not the one that's crazy."

"I lied to you," Minotti admitted, still amused. "I never fired this thing before. I was always afraid it might blow up on me."

Bolan told him, "Now's your chance to find out. And it really doesn't matter, does it?"

"I guess it don't," said Crazy Marco—not so crazy, after all.

He braced himself and squeezed into the trigger-pull. The .45-calibre weapon bucked and snorted, shaking Minotti's entire frame until he instinctively tightened into the grip and tucked the butt into his shoulder. Victoria went to hell in a hurry under the withering impact of that furious assault. Minotti was just getting into the spirit of the thing when Bolan reversed the Beretta and clunked it against the skull just behind the ear.

The firing ceased abruptly, the Thompson fell away, and Not-So-Crazy Marco slumped to the floor—unconscious but also not-so-dead.

As good as dead, of course, sure.

But Bolan had positive plans for this guy's final breath.

He holstered the Beretta, lifted the unconscious figure across the shoulders, and started out of there.

But then that Victorian door banged open and a Red Ace marked Donald Rutiglio danced inside with a long-barrel pistol in dangerous extension and a smug smile upon his face.

"You die, Omega," he declared softly, ". . . or Bolan, or whomever."

But Bolan Omega Whomever did not die, not there, not then.

The brief chatter of a light submachine gun, an Uzi if Bolan's perceptions were reliable, told the difference a split-second before the lights dimmed out within those Diamond eyes and a minor ace sagged into the discard pile.

Leo Turrin moved swiftly inside, turned the body onto its back with his foot, and quietly declared, "You were right, Sarge. You okay?"

"I'm fine, Leo," Bolan told that good friend. "You're the best flanker I've ever had."

Leo smiled—and then the hard men, the determined men, went outside to see what Central Park was like on a sunny Saturday afternoon.

CHAPTER 20

SATAN'S AFTERNOON

It was Saturday afternoon, yes, but not sunny, after all. A menacing line of thunderheads were approaching from the southwest, already blocking out the sun and sending their heavenly rumbles toward the city.

"I hope that's not an omen," Leo said, glancing at the sky.

"I hope it is," Bolan told him, smiling as he stepped aboard the Warwagon with his unconscious burden.

April greeted him with: "You always come in with something on your back. What is this? —bunkie day?"

He grinned at her, said, "You know what day

it is," and deposited Crazy Marco in the sleeping section.

Leo went aft to the armory and checked in his weaponry.

April moved to the con, tossed a questioning look at her man, then dropped onto the copilot's side. "The chief is waiting for us in the park," she said. "You know where."

Bolan knew where, yes.

The thing still was not sitting quite right in his belly—but the feds had set it up this way, so this was the way it would have to be.

He went to the con, slid in behind the wheel, and went to the rendezvous in the park.

These guys had a big thing going with do-it-yourself sawhorses—the type where pre-cut two-by-fours could be inserted into metal clamps for instant assembly, then taken apart again for easy storage. Even so, they must have been carting a truckload around with them. It appeared that an entire section of Central Park was now blocked off and closed to the public. The cover story was, of course, that a dangerous fugitive was loose and cornered in there—and there were plenty of city cops strolling around, too.

The marshals at the forward barricade recognized the Warwagon as it approached and hurried to open the way. Bolan breezed on through with a curt nod of the head to those solid men out there—most of whom, probably, were not

164

entirely sure of just what the hell was going down.

A jagged bolt of lightning streaked across the sky and, a moment later, the rain began again.

Bolan started the wipers and glanced at April. She was staring somberly ahead—thinking too, perhaps, of that which lay ahead and trying to get her head straight.

So was he.

Maybe Bolan would never see Central Park in the sun. For that matter, maybe he would never see it in the rain again, either. He was feeling philosophic, but not overly so—dreamlike, maybe, was the better word.

It had finally come down to this moment . . . this Saturday afternoon moment in Central Park —but it did not seem real, no. Maybe too much had gone before, or too much undone—maybe, okay, too much overdone. Whatever, there was no sensation here, now that the thing was done, the war behind him—but, for the first time since he'd stopped thinking about such things, there actually seemed to be a future in store for Mack Bolan.

Well, not really. For the flesh . . . but not for the name. Mack Bolan was going to die. He was scheduled to die on Saturday afternoon in Central Park.

It was sort of like going to one's own funeral.

He pulled the big cruiser to a halt at the designated spot. The rain was really coming down now, pelting the windowglass in a steady drumfire like hail. If there was anybody around, who would know?

The omen, sure. They were not always bad.

Then someone banged on the door. Bolan immediately hit the relay, the door opened itself, Hal Brognola leapt inside cursing.

He was not wearing a raincoat, or any protective gear. His suit was dripping water in puddles at his feet.

"Did you order this goddam weather, Striker?" he inquired with mock hostility.

"It's made to order, isn't it?"

The chief went to the bunk to peer closely at Minotti, then he came forward and opened a heavy briefcase at the plot table. "I've got the goods," he announced. "Do you have a towel? So I don't drip all over the damned . . ."

April brought a large bath towel and patted him down. She said, teasingly, "Don't say I never dried your back, Chief."

So that was good. She was back to the here and now, apparently in relatively good humor. Bolan squeezed her and brushed her forehead with a quick kiss. "Lose yourself," he suggested, making eyes toward Brognola's briefcase.

She threw him a go-to-hell look but obeyed immediately, moving back to the con with a flash of saucy eyes and swishing hips.

It was getting real now.

Brognola hauled out a pressboard binder containing a thick sheaf of documents held in place by Acco fasteners. "This is just a copy," he told Bolan, "so you can hang onto it and study it later. It's your official history, Colonel."

Bolan smiled soberly. "So I'm a colonel."

"You were," the chief replied, digging for other documents. "Now . . . John Phoenix is the name and chasing terrorists is the game. Don't worry, you're fully covered, fully documented. Everything you have there is also on file—the originals, of course—on file at the Pentagon. Fingerprints, dental records, medical reports, the whole smear has been transferred to the new file. Now . . ." He produced another "file" and showed it to Bolan. "Last chance to look it over, Sergeant. This was your life."

"Thanks," Bolan replied, a bit tightly. "I'll pass."

"Sure?"

"I'm sure."

"Okay." Brognola returned the file to the briefcase, sighed, cast a long look toward the sleep area. "We have all his vitals superimposed onto the old Bolan file. All identifying criteria. I guess we're ready."

Leo observed, "The guy is about a foot too short, Hal."

"Makes no difference," Brognola replied. "All the vitals for comparison are in the official record. Whatever they can lift from Marco can be verified by the Bolan file."

The subject of that talk, one of them, shifted uncomfortably, reached for a cigarette, changed his mind. "Do I smoke?" he asked with grim humor.

The chief said, "I hope you're not getting second thoughts."

"I've never lost them," Bolan told him. "But let's—"

"This was an excellent day, Striker!" Brognola testily reminded him. "I mean, every goal was realized. Except—well, I mean . . ."

"The kid," Bolan said quietly.

The official mien wavered, then broke apart. Brognola sat down, lit a cigar, offered one to Bolan, then growled, "No, hell, you don't smoke cigars," gave it to Turrin instead.

"Don't worry the kid," Bolan told the chief. "I believe I have the information."

"What do you have?"

"A presidential aide, Martin Thomas."

Brognola sighed. "That's the one, yeah. We got the make, too, just before I came over here. Uh, *the* man, himself, recognized the photos we faxed down. I mean, instant make. Now—I have good news and I have bad news. The good news, if you'll pardon a calloused heart, is that Marty Thomas is dead."

Bolan shot a strained look at Turrin and asked, "How'd he die?"

Brognola sighed. "He was confronted with the photos of his daughter. Excused himself, went into his bedroom, blew his brains out."

April had moved back to within good earshot, having recognized the nature of the discussion.

While Bolan and Turrin stared silently at each other, she said to Brognola, "If that's the good news, Chief, you know what you can do with your bad."

"Wish I could," he said, head bowed over the cigar.

"What is it?" Bolan asked.

"The kid died," Brognola muttered. "The pictures we sent were pictures of the dead."

Bolan got up and went to the con. He lit a cigarette, stared vacantly at the smoke arising from it, then went back to the quiet group at the plot.

Somehow there was no such thing as "insulation" in such matters—no matter how professional, no matter how often it occurs. And there was no such thing, either, as a "casual" relationship with a fifteen year old kid, however anonymous it may be. You touch them once, just once, in a hardrock situation and you immediately care how that situation works out.

They all had cared about that sick kid.

Bolan could understand Brognola's irritable, officious manner when first he came aboard. He touched the chief on the shoulder and said, "So who can say—maybe it's all for the best. Sounds like her world had already gone to hell around her, anyway."

Brognola said, "Yeah."

April told them all, "She had irreversible brain damage, that much I can tell you without a medical report. It's just almost inevitable in these cases."

The mood in there had gone from jittery to downright depressing. Leo noted it, saying, "Well, it's been that kind of day, hasn't it."

Bolan muttered, "Crazy Marco says the devil took it."

There was movement, back there, when he said that. Bolan caught Brognola's eye and sent the signal. The chief sighed heavily, looked knowingly at his three co-conspirators, and said, "Okay. I guess we all know what we have to do. Can we get it moving, now?"

Bolan went aft, checked his prisoner with a rough poke to the ribs, got no response whatever. "Marco will keep," he announced to the world at large. He went to the armory, picked up a pre-packed leather bag, carried it with him as he rejoined the others. "All I want is in here," he said. "April?"

"We took my stuff out this morning," she replied.

Leo was looking wistfully around at the impressive equipment in that good warship.

Brognola said to Bolan, "By the way, just a minute, that guy you wanted me to find—Gino—he's in the van. Locked up. You said special case. What's special?"

Minotti moved again.

Bolan dismissed it from his mind. He reached

into his bag and withdrew a heavy brown envelope. "I'm going to ask a personal favor, Hal," he said quietly. This was no "set-up," but for real.

Hal knew it. He replied, "It's about time. Ask it."

Bolan handed over the brown envelope. "Give this to Billy Gino. And cut him loose."

Brognola accepted the envelope, thoughtfully looked it over, asked, "What is it?"

"The last of Augie's money, bottom of my warchest. Not enough there to serve as a fitting pension for loyal service across the years but maybe enough for a new start somewhere. Billy is one of the last of the romantics, Hal. I'm sure he never did a rotten thing outside the families. He was the grounds cock for Augie the whole time he was in the outfit. If he ever killed, it was some savage trying for too big a bite from Augie's table. Cut him loose and send him south, far south. He was a gunner's mate, once, in the navy. Still likes boats. He should find one and make an honest living. Tell him I said it. I believe he will."

Brognola was making a sober smile. "How do you manage to know so much about these guys?"

Bolan tapped his forehead and replied, "*This* was my life, Hal. It's all there, indelibly. Take my word, Billy Gino is an okay guy. And I owe him one." He winked at Leo. "Hell, I owe him a couple."

171

Leo said, "He's right, Hal."

Brognola smiled, pocketed the envelope, stepped toward the door. "*Hard* man," he said sarcastically.

Bolan shrugged. "Hard doesn't mean brittle."

Brognola paused with his hand at the door. "You can begin the countdown whenever you're ready."

"You're sure it's clear?"

"There's not even a field mouse."

"Okay," Bolan replied. "It begins right now."

"See you tomorrow. In Wonderland?"

Bolan grinned, enclosed April and Leo in a tight circle of arms, and said, "We'll be there."

"Two o'clock sharp."

"Two it is. I, uh, notice you fixed it so I'll be introduced to the man, the first time, as Phoenix."

Brognola sent a wide grin from that doorway, said, "Well, that's politics," and went on out.

"I'll have a time getting used to that," said April.

"You like the sound of Bolan?"

"Not especially." She tossed her head and said, "I got used to the sound of Striker."

It was upon that light note that the three good friends descended from the only home Mack Bolan had known throughout much of his war. Bolan left the door agape and sent a final look inside.

Minotti was quiet.

Like a fox, yeah.

The rain was falling in buckets but Bolan did not even notice. He herded April and Leo to the limousine that awaited them, a hundred feet to the rear. A grinning marshal pushed the door open for them. April and Leo leaped inside immediately. Bolan leaned down to speak through the open doorway. "I'll wait out here," he told them.

"You'll catch your death!" April protested.

That was a good one.

It was precisely what he wanted to catch.

His wait in the rain was of short duration. The cruiser's big rear-mounted engine coughed softly to life and immediately it began to creep forward. Then the lights flared on and it leaped away.

Bolan reached into his pocket and withdrew a small black box, no larger than his palm.

He watched the lights of home until he could see them no longer, then he pushed a sliding switch forward and depressed a pushbutton.

The rainsodden park roared immediately with the fury of the auto-destruct system and the rain itself gave temporary right of way to trumpeting flames.

The secondaries began then, almost immediately, as the hot stuff in the armory joined the act.

It was a hell of a show. Too bad it was not Independence Day. But maybe it was . . . for someone.

He could see tomorrow's headlines in the eye of his mind, knowing what they would say and wondering what they would mean to the average man or woman on the street. Just another murderer, maybe, who got what he asked for.

It was true, of course. Only the names would be changed . . . to protect the nation, a soft nation going covertly hard.

As he watched, unashamed tears sprang from his ice-blue eyes and mixed with the raindrops to flow along that granite face—tears not for the likes, certainly, of a Crazy Marco with savage dreams but tears of gratitude to all those who had supported a weary soldier along the way, of pride and respect for some who had perished in the attempt—and sadness, yes—tears of an almost overpowering sadness for all the memories and sacred moments which were now boiling into the heavens as that gallant ship consumed itself.

Tomorrow would take care of tomorrow.

The devil himself had taken care of today . . . and today, thank God, had already ceased to exist.

Mack Bolan was dead forever.

EPILOGUE

The first page from John Phoenix's journal:
  Ashes to ashes and dust to dust. But how
  many men have known the privilege of
  rising from their own ashes, in the same
  time and place? Will this be a new beginning?—or will it be merely a continuation
  along the same pathways through hell? I
  guess the best that I can hope is that it
  will be another side of hell—a new neighborhood—with essentially the same focus as
  before. But I can bear it. A focus in hell
  is better than no focus at all—which, when
  you think about it, must be the worst of
  all possible hells. I will bear it, yes—until
  the last struggling ash settles finally into
  Mother Earth.

The Executioner explores a new hell in *Executioner* #39, coming to you from Pinnacle Books in October 1980.

the EXECUTIONER by Don Pendleton

Over 25 million copies in print!

———————— Clip and mail this page with your order ————————

PINNACLE BOOKS, INC., Reader Service Dept.
2029 Century Park East, Los Angeles, CA 90067

Please send me the book(s) I have checked above. Enclosed is my check or money order for $_____ (please add 75¢ to cover postage and handling).

Name _____

Address _____

City _____ State/Zip_____

ABCDEFGHIJKLMNOPQRSTUVWXYZ 12345678910